KU-750-134

Contents

Picnic at Asgard
Jenny T. Colgan

Monday 5 May 5147

Stormcage

'Oi!' was the first thing I heard.

This was a good sign. Definitely boded well. I risked cracking open an eyelid.

'What the blooming heck do you think you're doing?'

Trying not to throw up would have been the honest answer.

It was the Time Hopper. Traded it with Frodene in the showers for ninety-five sugar mice that had unaccountably arrived anonymously 4,600 years past their sell-by date; and an incredibly rare and holy protective relic Father Octavian sent me years ago, with a letter begging that I keep it by me always in my quest for true repentance. Frodene likes it glinting on her tail.

The Hopper can't get you past the Tesla force field, of course, but – if you're happy to stay in one place – amazingly, it works perfectly. Here I was, still in my cell, geographically perfect; but on the very day the cell was being built. The bars weren't even fitted yet.

'Where'd you spring from, then?'

I noticed the workman's surprised voice sounded slightly muffled, then realised to my annoyance that I couldn't breathe. They hadn't oxygenated the area yet. *So* annoying.

'Sorry! Gotta go!' I said in a slightly strangulated voice, quickstepping over his tools and stopping merely to grab his keycard and his oxygen supply.

I am almost one hundred per cent sure... maybe seventy-nine per cent sure... that one of his colleagues would have got to him with back-up oxygen in time.

And after that, we would both need a day off.

Asgard

He was waiting, arms folded, leaning against the TARDIS, pretending he wasn't fidgeting. He hates waiting. If he's not arriving in the nick of time, it isn't worth it.

'Come on!' he said. 'It's open and everything! We're missing it!'

'Hello, Sweetie.'

'I thought,' he said, unfolding his arms, 'you only called people that when you couldn't remember their names.'

'Not true,' I replied, ditching the stolen helmet. 'It's also if I can't remember their gender. Anyway, I had to stop at the market.'

He looked dubiously at the wicker basket I'd brought. 'What are we having to eat?'

'Stop being fussy.'

'I just want to—'

'No,' I said firmly. 'If you're picking the location, I'm picking the food. And, by the way, the location is *ridiculous*.'

He turned round, gleefully, the vast golden gates spread out before us, shining like mad in the morning sun. 'Isn't it?!'

ASGARD™. A planet-sized theme park. It is ridiculous. Beyond ridiculous. 'A celebration of all things legendary.' The skies were a heaving, rolling pink, always with a strategic ray of sun bursting through triumphantly; you could take part in a great fire funeral, or join the Beating Tunnel Ship of 10,000 Drums ride; or fly mechanical eagles through thrilling rock falls. They have a 5,000-metre waterfall with a hotel built into the cave behind it that's lit entirely by naturally occurring prisms.

'This place is so tacky,' I said, as we walked through the vast bright shining gates towards the Rainbow Bridge, with thousands of other excited-looking tourists; children bubbling with excitement, wearing their toy winged helmets and brandishing bendy hammers indiscriminately and then being told off for it.

'Don't anger the Gods!'

'Are you going to be like this all day?'

I nudged at him to look at the family near us. They were Pharax. Blue, at any rate. Three parents, and a clutch of children at various stages, including one nearly fully grown, and obviously a teenager. His clothes were ill-fitting and drooped, and he slouched, as much as a flint exoskeleton could slouch.

The lad's expression showed plainly how annoyed he was at being dragged here, even as his younger siblings bounced and hopped cheerfully round his feet and pointed at things they wanted to buy later. And he kept taking out an electronic device, whereupon one of his parents would tell him to put it away and he would scowl and do it reluctantly.

'Teenagers are the same in every galaxy,' I said.

'I know,' said the Doctor, smiling. 'Brilliant.'

And there was a slight pause. And I told myself sternly I wasn't bringing it up.

'Certainly, sir, madam,' the attendant in the booth was saying, as the Doctor waggled the psychic paper at him. 'It's a great honour to have you here today. Let me make sure you have VIP passes to everything. Gets you to the front of all the rides.'

'Oh,' said the Doctor, looking wounded. 'Oh, no, I mean, we would *never* push in in a queue.'

'Doctor!' I hissed. 'I'm not waiting for hours to go on stupid rides! Take the passes!'

'But it's not fair!' he said.

The attendant was beginning to look suspicious, which always has a wobbly effect on psychic paper.

'Just take them!' I said.

'And your complimentary horned helmets!' offered the attendant.

'No, thank you,' I said, at the exact same second the Doctor said, 'Cool!'

We joined the hordes of day-trippers streaming onto the Rainbow Bridge.

'I'm not skipping the queues, though,' he said mutinously.

'I know,' I said. 'That's why I brought a book.'

Still, you would have had to be a lot more churlish than me – and have spent a lot less time staring at a brick wall – not to be impressed by the Rainbow Bridge.

This area of the park was always a stunning gold and pink dawn, fresh fingers of the sun warming your shoulders; and a 5,000-piece orchestra played you across on great swells of sublime music. You could glimpse the endless waterfall in the distance, but the river below was wild and deep and clear and looked like the most refreshing, cold and delicious thing ever, like liquid sunlight. (They had glasses of it for sale at a concession stand, so you could find out – for an exorbitant fee.) Still, you really did feel like you were leaving one world behind, and I smiled, feeling quite excited.

'I'm not doing the mining,' I warned him.

'Come on! "Join 5,000 trolls digging for real gold and diamonds in a hundred real mountain tunnels a mere eagle ride away!"' the Doctor read from the map. 'What's not fun about that?'

'You're forgetting I only narrowly avoided the hard labour mines…' I began, but he'd gone. I glanced around. He'd better not be looking for trouble. This was not the day for that. Plus, I had to talk to him about …

I spotted him by the stone sides of the bridge, kneeling in front of a very small rotund humanoid child, who was sobbing inconsolably.

'It's OK,' he was saying. 'You're not lost. Well, not for long. Nobody can stay lost for long. Not when I'm about. Here, look at this.'

He took his screwdriver out and made it shoot tiny coloured fireworks in the air. Which I had thought was a waste of space when he did the modification, so shows all I know.

The child's eyes widened and it reached up a sticky hand.

'I know, it's my favourite, too,' said the Doctor. 'But don't touch. What's your mother's name? Do you know?'

'Mama,' said the child.

'Yes,' said the Doctor. 'Good start. Got anything else to go on?'

'Want Mama!'

'Let me just programme this to get a DNA trace—'

The child grabbed hold of the sonic very tightly and refused to let it go.

'The thing is, if you give it back to me, I can find your mama.'

'Find Mama!' ordered the child. 'Give LIGHTS ME! ME LIGHTS!'

'Let me just…' said the Doctor, switching the fireworks setting off.

'WAAAAH!!!!' The child screamed fit to wake the dead.

Suddenly a vast lumbering mountain of a person huffed over and grabbed the child by the hand.

'Mure! There are you are! Oi! What the blooming heck do you think you're doing?'

I was hearing that a lot today.

'Well, your child was lost, and I was—'

'He ain't lost!'

'But I was—'

'WANT LIGHT MAMMA!!!!'

'Give him that light, then.'

'But I was…'

'GIVE IT.'

'Manners…' said the Doctor weakly.

I stepped out in front. 'Excuse me,' I said, in a voice I have known to get excellent results. 'Were you planning to join in the funeral pyre ritual later? Because if you weren't, I'd be quite happy to facilitate it.'

'*River*,' said the Doctor.

The woman looked at me, sizing me up.

I smiled broadly, and pulled back my coat to give her a quick glimpse of my prison tattoo. (It's temporary: I needed to gain Frodene's trust. Well, I *hope* it's temporary.)

The woman balked and backed away. 'Well, you can see who wears the trousers with you two,' she spat, marching away. 'Come on, Mure.'

'What's wrong with wearing trousers?' asked the Doctor, puzzled. He said goodbye sweetly to the child, who was being roughly hauled away, great big puddles of bright snot pooling on his upper lip.

'Want light,' the boy hiccupped sadly, looking over his shoulder, as his mother shook him roughly, then jammed some sweets in his mouth.

I wondered. Now? Should I do it now? I couldn't stop thinking about it. This would have been the moment, I know. To ask him. Asking the Doctor for advice on my personal life. Oh lord, I have had better ideas.

The thing is, normally I love making him laugh, when I do things he wouldn't. But I am never truly as brave as I pretend to be, and, actually, I have a theory that he is absolutely the only creature in the universe who is.

Regardless: I couldn't bear the idea of him laughing *at* me.

I couldn't bear it. After all, with my childhood... imagine, me. The very idea of raising a child. Absurd. Who would leave a child with someone as dangerous as me? How would I have the faintest idea what to do: I who had known absolutely nothing of parenting. How could I tuck a child into bed?

And what if he thought I was asking him? That would be ridiculous. Completely stupid.

After all, what kind of father would he make anyway? He lives in the moment, only for today. That's what children do, not what they need. They need utter repetitive boredom, day after day after day, life exactly the same; a great big net of boring: of boring old love and times tables and vegetables. Nothing we could even begin to provide.

But if not now, when? Because I am not getting any younger.

Because he is.

Not that I am thinking about that.

'Hey!' I said, as something landed on my hair.

'You looked distracted!'

'That is absolutely no reason to fasten a helmet on me!'

'Chill out, Brunhilde!' the Doctor said. 'Now, there was a girl...'

'You know, Vikings didn't really wear horns on their helmets.'

'Mythic ones did,' he said, marching off, and the moment was gone.

The main square of Asgard™ was heaving; everywhere were half-timbered buildings; a working smithy – huge – where you could get weapons hammered into shape, or jewellery; there were bakeries selling honey cakes, and, obviously mead stalls everywhere. The Doctor couldn't stay still, zooming from one side of the square to another, cheerfully replying 'Hello!' back to grinning people who were clearly just being paid to say hello: it was all the same to him.

'Starting shortly in the Valhalla Amphitheatre: the fearsome Dragon Wars of Thor,' came a booming over the loudspeaker system. The crowds started to move in that direction.

'Ooh,' said the Doctor, looking at me expectantly. 'How can you *possibly* want to watch a fake animatronic monster show?' I said in disbelief.

'Are you kidding? Somewhere people are screaming at a monster and I don't have to do anything? Tremendous! Scream away! I shall have my feet up on the seat in front. Unless they tell me not to.'

And he led on, exuberantly. I wouldn't have told him so in a million years, but he rather suited the helmet.

The vast amphitheatre was crowded with people from all over the galaxy. I couldn't work out what the strange thing was I was feeling; then I realised. It was normality. Going to a theme park. For fun. With someone you cared about. Being hideously gouged for mead. I was enjoying all of it.

We were ushered to special VIP seats front and centre.

'VIP sucks!' shouted someone behind us, and we both looked embarrassed and agreed. I looked round. It was the grumpy teenager from before.

One of his triparents was trying to admonish him. I overheard him say, 'Well, if you hate all this stuff so much, you're more than welcome to go and get a job, Tomith.'

'Yeah, and end up like you?' The teenager sniffed and buried his head back in his device, completely ignoring what was taking place in front of him.

Which was a shame, as I have to admit, I have seen some sights, but the Asgard™ dragon show was quite the most spectacular.

First the orchestra played their most stirring music – and if you have never heard 3,000 violins play in harmony, I recommend it – then due to some clever atmospheric tweaking, the sun suddenly set above our heads in a million glowing shades of pink and purple streaking across a golden sky. As the stars popped out above us, thousands and thousands of tiny candles lit themselves, until the amphitheatre was a glittering fairyland and a collective 'ooo' could be heard from the crowd.

I realised we were holding hands, but we weren't running.

A man brandishing a huge sword ran onto the floor of the amphitheatre, holding up his weapon. He looked tiny down there. Then behind him came more and more and more; as the orchestra beat the drums, an entire army emerged, standards raised, marching in perfect unison to the music; it was oddly stirring, as thousands of them lined up, displaying their marching skills. Then the music changed, and lots of women ran on too, with long plaits and beautiful embroidered garments, and the entire arena erupted into a victory war dance around the campfires which sprang up suddenly.

Then just as we were lulled into the display, a single person, dressed in furs, tore onto the floor. He could have been an interloper, except for his sword, and he shouted loudly about a dragon, a dragon coming this way, whereupon the actors dissolved their dancing and made a huge line; brought out their weapons which all burst into huge lines of flame above their head, and the music changed to something ominous and scary.

There was a long pause and then a great noise, like a huge metal foot striking the ground.

'Oooh!' said the Doctor. 'What's that?'

There was another sound, then another, then another from near the entrance. The crowd of performers shrank back, and so did the audience. And when the burst of flame appeared, everybody jumped. It was immense; we could feel the heat from up in the box.

'Whoa!' said the Doctor.

Then BOOM you could just see, entering the arena, one huge metal claw. The ground shook. Then another, then another; clang clang clang. The Doctor was gripping me in excitement. Then there was a huge cloud of smoke across the arena and when it cleared, the creature was there, at least four storeys high; a genuine metal monstrosity, shaped like a dragon, with huge bright red glowing eyes. It opened its sharp jaws wide to the sky and an enormous roar and a billowing flame erupted.

The beast rampaged around the stadium floor, causing the performers to cower in terror; occasionally approaching a bank of the audience. At one point it reached out a surprisingly delicate claw and lifted a hat off someone, to vast applause.

Then the mood darkened again; the people on stage cowered, and in another puff of smoke, from the entrance appeared a man – a huge man, blond of hair and beard, incredibly over-muscled (*some* might say), dressed in chainmail and a loin cloth, with a hammer the size of me, marched into the arena to a huge and overwhelming standing ovation from the audience.

'Why do I never get one of those?' came the voice to my left.

'Sssh,' I said. 'It's just getting interesting. He's very oily.'

'Fierce and mighty dragon!' shouted Thor, amplified throughout the arena. 'Face me in combat!'

The dragon turned round, its red eyes blinking, smoke puffing from its giant nostrils. With a roar it pawed the ground and prepared to charge. Thor stood his ground. It looked a ridiculously uneven fight, as the dragon backed the man into a corner, whereupon Thor struck the weapon with an almighty clank, and harmless green sparks showered the first ten rows. He swung it round with some rather unnecessary pyrotechnics, then whacked it straight into the head of the dragon, which staggered backwards, then regrouped to run at him again. But now Thor was a blur of motion; spinning and hacking; at one stage seemingly cornered, then rolling out from underneath the creature; temporarily losing his sword, but not before he'd hacked off a great sharp-needled toe from the dragon and was fighting him off with his own pointed nail, etc. It was all very stirring stuff; the dragon veered almost but not too dangerously close to the crowd; just at the last minute, the flames wouldn't quite reach, or the claws would draw back, as the audience screamed.

Thor was gearing up for the very last charge; the audience in a frenzy. He had escaped near-death several times now and the crowd was absolutely ready for the kill. He advanced slowly on the puffing, bucking, crazed animatronic beast.

And then something strange happened. The tail of the dragon went over the side of the barrier, and knocked an entire row off their seats. A great screaming broke out. The huge beast wobbled and wavered as if about to topple over, and absolute panic broke out in the stands. We both stayed watching closely, neither of us sure whether or not this was all part of the act; perhaps that section of the audience were stooges, to make the experience more intense for the spectators. Then the Doctor grabbed my arm.

'Look,' he said.

The dragon was now twirling around, its robotic limbs flailing everywhere, and it had inadvertently scooped up a figure from the stands.

It was a child; the same child we'd found earlier, wandering free from its parents. It had clearly been wandering free again, and had got onto a very dangerous path.

The dragon lurched, holding the tiny child – who looked even tinier in its claws – as the audience screamed and gasped.

'Quick…' I said, turning, but of course the Doctor had already gone.

There must have been a control room somewhere, because the dragon lurched to the left and to the right as there was a frantic struggle for control. And as people started to dangerously cram themselves towards the exits in panic, and the actors vanished, I saw a lone lanky figure down on the floor of the amphitheatre, waving his arms.

The beast was a robot of course, it had no independent thought at all, but it responded to movement and noise. I ran down the steps towards the stage and clambered over the barriers. Security had vanished, which was a tad disappointing. Perhaps all that smiling had tired them out.

The Doctor was trying to get close to it, but every time he approached, the dragon would drop its head and make a lunging noise, just as it was programmed to do so with Thor, who was, I noticed disapprovingly, huddled in a side entrance, pressed against the wall, terrified. He'd left his hammer discarded in the middle of the stage.

'I'll distract it!' I shouted, hoping the hammer would have a trigger effect on the robot, which it did. I couldn't lift it, but I could waggle it from side to side. The robot turned its mighty head towards me.

'Give him one of your looks,' came the Doctor's voice as he charged round the back of the great beast and tried to grab it by the tail, which lashed furiously.

The child was screaming, but seemed to be being held quite securely. I didn't have a hope of reaching up there, and wished I still had my trusty lasso. Instead, I glanced around. There were stones on the ground, surrounding the facsimile campfires. I picked them up and tried to figure out where to throw them that wouldn't hit the howling boy. I aimed for the knees, which seemed to work; the creature started to unbalance slightly, leaning, then overreaching.

'Again!' shouted the Doctor.

I let loose and the great tail came crashing down for long enough for him to grab hold of it. He clambered up it, carefully, as I stopped throwing stones – I didn't want the beast to fall with the two of them on it, and instead ran underneath, trying to work out where best to place myself if I had to catch the child.

The Doctor was now hoisting himself up the underside of the creature's tail, so it looked as if he were hanging off a giant branch, and was pulling himself hand over hand.

'Help!' the woman was screaming from the sidelines. 'GET MY BABY!'

I watched the Doctor and the boy anxiously, adrenalin pounding, as the Doctor shouted, 'Right! On my count, River, be ready!'

And with an almighty lunge, he let go with both hands, with only his legs clinging on to the rampaging creature's tail, and hurled himself backwards. The creature lurched, the leg I'd damaged moving up in the air – then, crack, there was the noise of a great switch being flicked, and the huge beast froze.

So did everybody fleeing for the exits. A momentary hush descended. But not for long.

There was an ominous creak. I held my breath. And the great four-storey creature twitched, just a little. And the leg I had whacked with stones started to tremble. It was like watching a tree being cut down.

The great stampede of people turned tail yet again and fled for the exits. We, on the other hand, could do nothing but stand and watch.

I drew a deep breath and stood as tall as I was able. Then I shouted at the child: 'Mure! Mure! Can you jump?'

The kid gazed at me with terrified eyes, shaking his head tightly.

'Jump to me,' I said. 'Come on, sweetie. You can do it.'

He shook his head mutely. The beast's leg trembled again. Inside there was a twisting noise of crunching metal. Something was going terribly wrong in there.

'You have to!' I said. 'Come on, Mure. You have to. Just do it!'

He shook his head again.

'Come on!' I shouted desperately. 'Come on! You can do it!'

The little boy edged slightly closer to the edge of the creature's great claws.

'That's right!' I said. 'Come on! I know you're very brave, and I'm going to catch you!'

He inched forwards a tiny bit more, and I smiled encouragingly.

'Come on!'

He was ready, his hands going up.

Suddenly his mother was by my side.

'MURE!' she screamed. 'GET DOWN HERE! GET DOWN RIGHT NOW!'

This had the opposite effect. The child shrank back into himself straightaway.

'NOW!'

The headshaking had recommenced. I glanced at the beast. Yes, the creaking was getting louder. The beast was starting to lean further and further over. I held my hands out even higher for the child.

'Mure. Please,' I said. It was such a long drop, and he was such a small child.

'River! Use this!'

The Doctor was sliding down the creature's tail, which had the unavoidable effect of unbalancing the beast completely. As he did so, he hurled his sonic high in the air, and it curled over the dragon's flanks and flew straight towards me.

I caught it in my left hand, and switched it up; the fireworks began to dance lightly from the end.

'Look, Mure!' I said. 'Look!'

And the huge beast began to topple, just as the little boy gazed at the fireworks, and shouted 'Lights!', and the Doctor leapt first, and was there supporting me, just as Mure leapt into my arms, as the robot landed on the arena floor with a crash that shook the earth.

Mure propelled us both back onto his mother, who took more than the brunt of it, but neither of them cared; she grabbed the child and smothered him in a mixture of hard hugs and kisses. The huge robot lay motionless and lifeless, half a section of seats completely squashed beneath it.

'Thank you, River and Doctor, for saving my baby,' said the Doctor pointedly.

'You're very welcome, polite and attentive parent,' I said, dusting myself down. 'You know, I think I'm going to leave it to you to retrieve the screwdriver.'

Outside, there were people screaming and rushing for the exits. We marched through them, looking for the Command Centre. We found it behind another beautiful village square, with its thatched roofs and half-timbered tumbledown houses and picturesque blondes performing an apparently traditional dance which involved quite a lot more exposed flesh that one would expected that far up in a planet's northern hemisphere, but that's a post-Earthly fantasy paradise for you.

If you crept round the back of the town square, though, there was a high thicket of trees, facilities for a variety of biologies; and a very small, unsignposted path. We looked at one another and nodded.

The Command Centre was an unobtrusive grey bunker, without windows, and several control panels on the roof. There was a keypad by the door and as we approached, several dark-suited people marched sharply up towards it and keyed it open, and we simply slunk in behind them.

Inside was a vast space down a flight of stairs; it must have extended underneath the park. Which made sense. Indeed as I looked around the huge underground control centre I saw, amongst myriad screens and working computers – and a big smiling 3D picture of Thor exhorting the staff to 'FIGHT WIN SMILE!' – were long tunnels, careering off everywhere, with little white travel cable pods, moving at remarkable speeds, delivering Vikings, dancers, cleaners, catering staff, who waited for the subway system like oddly dressed commuters, presumably so nobody had to watch Thor queue for the toilet. It was quite a sight.

'Who are you?' said an unfriendly voice. I looked up. The voice belonged to a species I didn't recognise, but looked a bit like a beaver. It was humanoid size though, and stood on two stilt-like legs, it was kind of cross and cute-looking all at once.

'Hullo!' said the Doctor. 'We're on the VIP tour! This bit's great!'

'No you're not,' said the beaver. An outbreak of shouting was taking place over by a bank of monitors. 'Now, clear out, this is a restricted area.'

He folded his tiny paws, not very impressively, although his expression was serious, as was the blaster tucked into the pocket of his frankly adorable beaver overalls.

'Out!'

The commotion got louder.

'Did you see those guys on the screen?' came a voice. A smaller, greyer creature – more mole-like, although with the same augmented limbs – came clattering over. 'They saved a kid in the crowd! We should give them an award or something. Actually, you know what, boss, having an event that almost goes horribly wrong and then comes good at the last minute... that might be an idea you know. Might add a good level of jeopardy to the crowd...'

HIs voice petered out as he took us in standing in front of him.

'And here you are!'

'It's a small world, after all,' said the Doctor.

'Well done, you guys.'

The beaver scowled and reviewed the monitors. 'Was that you?'

'Saved the day!' said the Doctor. 'Where were security, by the way?'

The beaver frowned. 'Helping people towards the exits. Preventing a panic. Exactly what they're meant to be doing.'

The beaver, the mole and I peered round the cavern. People were yelling and dashing around.

'Glad to see there's no more panic… I'm the Doctor, by the way.'

'And I'm the Professor,' I said, smiling politely.

'So. What happened to your dragon?' asked the Doctor.

The beaver sniffed. 'I'm Caius Roose. Park Director,' he said. 'And it's nothing to worry about. Small mechanical failure. All fixed now.' He glanced at me. 'Are you one of the Brunhildes?'

'Enough of that.'

'Cause you sound just like her.'

The Doctor looked around. 'Are you going to close the park?'

Caius shook his head. 'Naw, just a minor technical issue. No one got hurt.'

'We should close it,' said the mole. 'Double-check everything.'

'I agree,' said the Doctor.

Caius scratched his head. 'We can't,' he said. 'It's our busiest time in the year. We close the park, we lose our profits, then next thing you know word gets out we're dangerous, and before you know it everyone stays away and we're out of business.'

'Maybe that's because you *are* dangerous,' I said.

'It's one mechanical failure,' muttered Caius again.

'We should still failsafe,' said the mole.

Caius turned on him. 'Postumus Fearne!' he said, exasperated.

'I'm just saying!' said the Mole.

'How many kids you got at home, Postumus?'

'Eleven,' said Postumus fondly.

'Right. And what are they going to eat when they find out Daddy's lost his job?' Caius turned back to us. 'There's 76,000 people work in Asgard™.'

He gestured a paw towards the long lines of people queuing for the subway trains, scooping them away, another tired-looking horde alighting as the cars stopped.

'It's a major source of employment in a very depressed part of the galaxy. And I'm responsible for them.'

'And for them,' said the Doctor, showing the screens that covered all of the park. Everywhere were happy youngsters out strolling with their families; with horned shaped balloons; babies in buggies; people having wonderful days in the sunshine.

'That's right,' said Caius. 'And look: there's no panic. Because everything is fine. And we'll investigate the mechanical fault and then everything can carry on just as it was.'

He looked around.

'I have the finest team in the galaxy, Doctor,' he said. 'Thanks for your help just now, but I'm not shutting this place down and sending them out to starve without a very good reason. Off with you now please. I only ask nicely once.'

Postumus showed us the door. His whiskers looked defeated.

'Postumus... do *you* think it's just a mechanical failure?' asked the Doctor quietly on the way.

Postumus glanced around. 'That should... it just shouldn't happen,' he said. 'I mean, it's the most sophisticated technology available. Should be unbreakable. I mean, it wouldn't just be an error. It wouldn't.' He fingered the pens in the top pocket of his dungarees. 'It's not how we do things at Asgard™,' he said. 'It just isn't. This is the happiest place in the galaxy.'

The Doctor raised an eyebrow. 'Now, where have I heard that before?'

Postumus accompanied us out the back way, and we emerged into the more sublime landscape of the park at large. We blinked in what was once again bright mid-afternoon sunshine. Above us circled lazy great golden eagles, which could be harnessed and ridden; ahead, grazing in a beautiful, endless elysian fields were the winged white Valkyrie horses, saddled up at night for the spectacular northern lights display that ended each day at the park.

There were signposts to the 'Enchanted Forest' ahead that led to, eventually, the great feasting halls of Valhalla, that supplied mead and sweetmeats at any hour of the day or night.

The Doctor looked back at the small door to the Command Centre, even now fading away between the trees.

'Those subways... they go all round the park, right?' Postumus nodded.

'So if we wanted to get in and have a better look without Caius setting any furry goons on us...'

Postumus looked even more worried. 'Look,' he said. 'He's tough, but he's a good boss, Caius. I wouldn't want to get into trouble or anything.'

'No, no, I realise that,' said the Doctor. 'But you think there's something wrong, don't you?'

Postumus nodded. 'Try under the great feasting halls of Valhalla,' he whispered. 'There's so many caterers and performers coming out of there all hours of the day and night, they'd barely notice you. Especially you...' He pointed at me. 'All you need is the metal breastplate.'

'*I don't look like...*' I started, as the Doctor smiled triumphantly, and I gave up. Instead, we set off towards the Enchanted Forest through the once more cheerful throng.

Following the path through the forest was curious. Firstly, no matter how many thousands of people approached the narrow dirt path at the same time, as soon as you entered the trees, everyone was completely dispersed so you couldn't see anyone in front or behind you; you felt completely alone.

Secondly, we entered the forest in early summer, hot yellow sun filtering through bright young green leaves, waterfalls tinkling with snow melt; and timid fawns scampering out of our way as we approached; but as we progressed, the leaves turned a darker and darker green, then began to coil up into themselves; to turn bright shades of yellow, red and orange; then they started to tumble down off the trees, and grouse took off into the sky, and the air became crisper, with the scent of bonfires in the air, and the sun turned mellow and golden and mists coiled along the bottom of the leaf- strewn path, as we kicked our way through them, speaking of what might have gone wrong with the park, and this and that, and he lent me his elbow, and I took it.

Do it, I told myself. Do it now. We were perfectly alone, perfectly peaceful. And the crunching leaves beneath my leather boots had turned, I noticed, to crunching snow, and the air was suddenly twilight and chill, the first flakes, now. swirling down, two snow-geese taking off above our heads, silhouetted against a newly minted moon; and I leaned in closer to him – he never feels the cold.

Just ask him, I told myself. It's not like he's not used to questions.

'Oh, look over there!' he said suddenly, just as I opened my mouth to speak. A gap in the trees had appeared, and I could see the snow-capped mountains of Asgard to the North – floodlit, and filled with gleeful skiers careening downhill, shouting and yelling in excitement.

'I've always wanted to try that. I should think I'd be very good.'

I burst out laughing. 'Don't be daft, your centre of gravity is far too high. You'd look like Crazy Legs the Crane. Anyway,' I continued. 'Look, there's something... something I need to ask you, and I don't even know if it's theoretically possible, and it's not even about you... probably... but if you thought no I need to see how that feels, and if it's yes I'd need to see how that feels, but I just need to ask, just once, and I have no one else to ask and... Do you think one day... I mean... I mean, one time. Do you think we... I... I might... do you think I might ever...'

Then there was a small blip, like I'd blinked a moment too long, and suddenly he was brushing snow off his jacket shoulders.

'Sorry,' he said. 'Lost concentration for a sec. What were you saying?'

I dropped his arm and stared at him. 'What did you just do?'

'Nothing.'

Something glinted inside his jacket. I grabbed at it. 'What's this?'

It was a gold medal. Inscribed on it was 'Helsinki, 1952'.

I looked at him for a long time.

'So what were you going to ask me?'

'Nothing,' I said. 'Forget it.'

I stomped off through the blizzard.

'Hang on, River!' he shouted after me. 'I can't run, my knees are shot.'

I did not 'hang on' and was almost out of the forest. Already I could see the braziers lighting the way to the palace of Valhalla up ahead, sending their flames high into the night.

And I could hear screaming.

The Palace of Valhalla looked like an optical illusion, because it was. It was tower upon tower, in thick grey granite; it resembled a great cathedral organ. Hundreds of windows were lit with thousands of glittering candles; you could enter any one of the 540 huge wooden doors.

I couldn't figure out where the screaming was coming from. A great smell of roasting meat and mead came towards us. I didn't notice this at first; for I was also dealing with the confirmation of something I knew all along: of course neither of us were remotely fit for parenthood. And I was an idiot even for thinking it, and wouldn't again.

We ran along the frosted path to the bottom of one of the towers. A girl in a metal breastplate lay unconscious on the ground; still breathing. She had the white cloak of one of the Valkyries; she was very young, and heavily made up. Her long wig lay in the snow. I knelt beside her, but as I did so, a troupe of security rushed up with a stretcher and erected a tent around her. 'Move along, please, she's fine, she's fine,' said a large mouse-like creature bossily. 'Just an accident. We do warn people not to run on the battlements.'

In an instant, she was whisked away, into one of the many doors in the walls.

'Another accident, huh?' said the Doctor. 'It does seem very careless, this place.'

We followed through the door through which they'd just disappeared; but we found ourselves in a huge hall, with only one set of doors.

I couldn't see how a stretcher could possibly have just come through here: inside, everyone was partying. The room was obviously an inter-dimensional trick: it contained a great long wooden table that went on for so far, the sightlines converged.

Everywhere along it were different families and groups together, eating, drinking happily, laughing and of course, making great toasts. Every so often there were huge fireplaces, above which meat was turning on spits, covered in herbs. Serving staff refilled goblets from huge, never-ending pitchers of mead.

'Ah,' said the Doctor.

He walked out, then came in again.

'What did you do that for?'

'No,' he said, gloomily. 'I came in a different door. Try it.'

I did so, and found myself exactly where I'd just been standing.

'A dimensional extension,' he said. 'Well, how else would you feed half a million visitors an hour, and make them all feel they're in the same great hall? They'll have gone somewhere else altogether.' He looked round. 'Something's very wrong here. What is it? Let me think.' He lifted a goblet of mead from a passing tray, drank it in one, then made a face.

'*Sip* stuff if you don't know you're going to like it!' I said crossly. I was about to try one for myself when one of the serving girls came running up to me.

'You're meant to be downstairs!' she hissed. 'The second show's about to start.'

The Doctor raised his eyebrows at me.

'*Fine*,' I said, as the girl pressed a carved wooden rose inlaid next to the fireplace, and a previously unnoticed door slid open in the wall. I followed her as we descended the steps to the corridors below.

Downstairs, everything was organised chaos. Thousands of identically clad wench-like girls were grabbing plates of hot meat and huge jugs of mead from a vast dispensing fountain – I rather liked that – in a complex but effective pattern.

Everything was hot and shouty, and I wandered into an endless kitchen full of workers of every conceivable stripe, hollering. They barely glanced up at me, and then I found a dressing room full of crying Valkyries, which led to an underground stables, full of pawing horses.

The girls asked me if I was Calinth's replacement and I said yes, and took the breastplate and the sword they gave me – it was a rather fine specimen – then I marched on, until I reached a side door marked 'Security', where I saw an empty stretcher.

'Excuse me,' I said, walking in. 'What's going on?'

'You can't be in here,' shouted someone.

'Really?' I said, fingering the sword. 'Well, tell me what's going on with Calinth and I'll leave quietly.'

A familiar furry figure stepped up, his whiskers twitching slightly.

'No, no, it's all right, Tullus,' he said. 'She's on our side.' He looked around. 'You've disconnected the cameras, right?'

'What's happening?'

Postumus looked crestfallen. 'It's the dimensional calibrator,' he said. 'Now somebody's messing with it.'

'Messing with it how?' I said.

'Well, it's carefully calculated, so everyone gets their Valhalla dining experience, whenever they want it. But someone's started folding the dimensions in. That poor girl was standing in a room that suddenly winked itself out of existence. She fell out of nothing.'

I blinked.

'She's going to be OK, though,' he added.

'And you don't know who would do that?'

The mouse called Tullus looked up. 'We love this place,' he said, and the others snuffled agreement.

'I need the Doctor,' I said.

I'd expected him to be doing what he usually did: making friends with everyone and becoming the centre of attention whilst pretending that sort of thing didn't matter to him.

Instead, he was sitting sulkily on the side by himself, pushing some food around his plate.

In front of the fire, an armoured chap with a huge glittering spear was roaring, 'So Odie, I said. So, Odie, let me tell you a thing or two about the bridge between the worlds. I mean, my bro and I got beef!' and the audience was either falling about laughing or hanging on to his every word.

'What's up with you?' I hissed.

'Well, he looks nothing like me, for starters,' said the Doctor crossly.

'Why would he?' I asked surprised.

'Oh, *no reason*,' he said. 'Just, you know. Mythological shapeshifter from ancient Earth history? Wears many faces? Plays tricks?'

I turned to him. 'That actor is meant to be playing *you? You're* Loki?'

'Credit where credit's due, that's all I'm saying. I was there. And *he's* a ham.'

'You're a ham,' I pointed out. 'Also he's very good-looking.'

'Do you really think so?' said the Doctor, brightening up.

'Anyway, that's not the point,' I said, and explained that someone had messed with the dimensional calibrator.

He turned ashen immediately and leapt to his feet.

'Is that bad?'

'Bad? It's… River, of course it's bad. It's like pulling a thread… you can't just tinker with a dimensional calibrator…'

And just as he said this, something started to shift. Just a very tiny amount, hardly at all. Blink and you'd miss… suddenly, there were two Lokis. And two tables. The great fire suddenly subdivided into two fires, catching a passing server, whose sleeve caught fire. She screamed.

Then there were more tables, and more, with people crowding out.

'We have to get them out!' shouted the Doctor, beating out the girl. 'It'll start to fold in on itself.'

Terrified staff were running in from secret doors all over the place, trying to get the crowds to muster and leave by the great doors.

I went to the great door. But as it opened I saw it opened not onto the outside, but instead into another great hall, with another Loki and another set of terrified people, trying to leave by another door, and yet another beyond. It had become an endless hall of mirrors.

Worse: the great fire that had caught the serving girl, had now caught the tapestries. The flames were ripping up the walls. Not just in our hall, but in every hall.

'It'll collapse in on itself,' shouted the Doctor, 'and leave nothing but the fire! We have to get these people out of here!'

The fire was licking at the straw roof of the great hall, even as the people were now cowering under the tables.

'Shield maiden,' said the Doctor, looking straight at me.

I looked back at him and nodded, and ran to the door. I pressed the carved wooden rose, and then we were down below, with staff running here and there in panic. We ran straight through the kitchen, where the mead was already beginning to bubble worryingly, and on to the dressing room.

'Sister Valkyries!' I shouted. The girls were cowering in the corner; their horses beyond whinnying and stamping in distress. The dimensional folding was happening here too; the stables went back and back and back.

'Now we go save them!' I shouted, holding up my sword.

They looked at me, astounded and terrified.

The Doctor didn't waste a moment, and swung himself onto the back of the nearest horse. I heard him whisper, 'What's your name? Oh, sorry, I forgot you're a robot.'

Then I followed suit. I turned to the girls. 'FOR WE ARE TRUE VALKYRIES,' I hollered at them, 'AND YOU WILL FOLLOW YOUR BRUNHILDE!'

And, astonishingly, they mounted their own horses and followed us.

Then we were off; clattering through the kitchen; bursting through the door into the great hall. The horses knew what they were programmed to do, and in that vast space, they took off, their wings flapping. It was the most astonishing feeling. I glanced over at the

Doctor, who grinned back at me; he was enjoying it as much as I was.

We circled the hall, then he broke through the smouldering hay into the starry night beyond and I followed.

Below us the great palace of Valhalla was an endless city now; rooms upon rooms upon rooms; an Escher jumble of the near-infinite.

Except behind us, up flew the other Valkyries through the roof; bold and strong and fearless; and from every other roof in every other iteration flew a line of Valkyries too; and we all banked sharply and flew down, scooping up the people in our own version of the great hall; one by one, or two by two, or in the case of a particularly small family from Junveres, seventeen by seventeen; we lifted them onto the backs of our winged horses, flew them up through the flaming roof under the great white winter moon and set them down gently on the great golden fields of Freyr the harvest goddess, beneath the bright freezing stars.

Just as we rescued the very last of the people from the great hall, the Doctor shouted, and I raised my sword in the air for everyone to stop. There was a vast, teetering silence from the herd of horses in the sky; even the hordes of frightened people in Freyr's fields held their breath.

Then, with a huge creaking noise, one, then another, then another hall folded into itself completely, like a house of cards, one by one by one, until they had all collapsed; folded themselves up and completely disappeared, leaving only the bare ugly network of tunnels and subways of Asgard™ beneath.

The crowd cheered as we set down the last of the rescued and dismounted, but the Doctor had no time; he was scanning the faces.

'Who did this?' he demanded. 'Who? Because people work really hard for their holidays, and you're just… you're just spoiling everything.' He stalked the hordes. 'Have you any idea how much we need a holiday? I'm travelling the universe and she's in PRISON.'

Everyone stared at me and I pretended to be very busy and distracted.

'… and I bet you all have the same thing. Just one day. To get away from your normal routine. To remember how much you love your family. To escape that feeling that everything is collapsing around your feet. And then it collapsed around your feet. And I think somebody here is responsible…'

There was suddenly a bolting figure from the back; a bright flash of blue, taking off towards where the tunnels began.

We turned and ran, chasing it. So did Postumus, who had reappeared, and moved remarkably fast on those long limbs of his.

Beneath the tunnels, everything was dank and utilitarian. We followed some very swift running feet.

'This way!' shouted Postumus, whose ears were pricked up. We followed him, the pathway twisting and turning and getting deeper.

Suddenly I clanked against something, and I nearly tripped. My leg was caught. 'What's that?'

'Oh, yeah,' puffed Postumus. 'That's the monorail. For the transportation pods.'

'The *what*?' I said. But it was too late. Already, I could see a gleam of light ahead, as one of the little pods was heading straight for us.

'Get into the side, River!' shouted the Doctor.

But I had seen something – something just ahead.

'It's blue!' I shouted. 'Get the guy! He's blue!'

I couldn't move my leg. The train was coming closer and closer. It didn't appear to have a driver.

'Go on!' I shouted. 'Get him!'

But the Doctor stopped running and turned back towards me; they both did. And both Postumus and the Doctor instantly gave up their quarry and came towards me and, with an extremely ungracious 1-2-3 HUMPH, quickly pulled me out of my boots. The Doctor heaved me first and rolled with me to the left side; Postumus made a dive to the right and, to our utter horror, didn't make it in time.

The white pod rolled past and over him, and, just underneath it, we saw one little paw, lying limp on the rail.

We dived back down to the track. Postumus was lying, eyes shut. His legs were horribly mangled. I stroked his very soft fur. Then I looked up.

At the end of the passageway, there stood a tall blue, humanoid shape, outlined in the lights.

I leapt up and pulled out my sword. 'And now,' I shouted, 'I believe you harmed a friend of mine.'

I stalked up the tunnel, sword trained on his chest.

As I drew closer, however, I noticed something. The figure wasn't trying to escape or attack. And yes, it was tall: but it wasn't a man. It was an overgrown child; it was the teenager we had noticed earlier; his gadget dangling from his fingers. Also, he was crying.

'I didn't mean it,' he sobbed, his mouth a wobbly line. 'I didn't mean it, but…'

'I've got a pulse!' shouted the Doctor, as I led the boy back down the tunnel at the tip of my sword.

'And I've got a miscreant. Did you just perform mouth to mole?' I said.

'It's not so bad once you get used to it,' said the Doctor, wiping his lips.

Postumus's eyes began to flicker.

'What… what happened…?'

I stroked his nose. 'It's all right,' I said. 'You've hurt your legs. But we'll get help.'

He nodded. 'They won't hurt,' he whispered. 'Do you know, they're actually augmented legs.'

'I absolutely hadn't noticed,' I whispered back, and he smiled.

And then, thankfully, the ambulance arrived, and transported us back to the central base.

All the lights were on in the control room, screens showing a rapidly emptying park. Postumus was propped up. Caius was marching up and down in front of the boy, who was apparently called Tomith, and his quivering parents.

'What on earth were you thinking?' he was shouting. For something that looked like a beaver, he was actually quite scary. 'You killed people! You nearly killed my staff! You could have killed everyone in that hall.'

Tomith was staring at the ground, trembling. 'I didn't mean any harm.'

'Oh, you didn't mean any harm,' said Caius. 'You might have destroyed this place for ever, you know that?'

'I was just hacking. Your security systems are so simple.'

The bristles went up on the back of Caius's neck. 'They're the finest on the market today!'

'Well, they're still terrible,' said Tomith. 'But I didn't… I didn't realise that would happen if you messed with the dimensional calibrator.'

'A little knowledge,' said the Doctor.

'You know the sentencing in this part of the world for hacking?'

One of Tomith's triparents burst into tears.

Tomith trembled even harder. 'I'm so so sorry. I've got exams and everything back on Nurfer. I'm really, really sorry, Sir.'

'You'll be even more sorry when you're on Death Row.'

The parent now looked close to collapse.

Tears ran down Tomith's face. 'I only wanted to mess with it a bit.'

'Well, you messed with the wrong theme park.'

'How old are you?' said the Doctor.

'Fifteen,' said the boy, or that's what the TARDIS translated for me.

The Doctor raised his hands up. 'He's a child, Caius.'

'He's a criminal child.'

'If I were you, I'd give him a job.'

'What?!'

'Sort out your security breaches once and for all. Poacher turned gamekeeper… No offence,' said the Doctor, looking round at the assorted woodland animals. 'Because it seems to me, Caius, you need a new perspective.'

'But he's going to be prosecuted…'

'You have children, Caius?'

Caius shrugged. 'Yeah,' he said.

'And how do you think they're going to feel when their dad loses his job for letting his park be destroyed… Or perhaps it stood up to a major test incident. And learned how to pass it… to make it truly secure.'

'I could do that,' gulped Tomith. 'I could!'

One of the triparents nudged another. 'A job!' they said in astonishment.

The Doctor moved closer to Caius. 'Could you send one of your own children to their death? For breaking the rules?'

'They wouldn't do anything like this.'

'Is there anything they could do, Caius? That could make you send them to their deaths?'

There was a long silence in the room.

Then Caius waved his paws in a gesture of dismissal. 'Fine,' he said. 'Postumus, can you handle it? If I promote you to Head of Security?'

'When I get my new legs, I will,' said Postumus, looking delighted.

Tomith couldn't believe his luck. A parent started singing a Pharax song of profound gratitude that wasn't particularly welcome. And the Doctor gave Tomith a look.

'You channel those enormous brains,' he said severely. 'Don't you dare get in trouble again. Don't you dare let your parents down like that.'

'I won't,' stammered Tomith, in tears of relief now. 'I promise, I won't, Sir. I'm so sorry. I'm so, so sorry.'

And he broke down again, and the Doctor ruffled his hair.

Oh, and then it hit me like a rock in the guts.

Not that it was any business of mine. But that was what he would be like as a father.

And what do I know? Maybe he does it already. Maybe they're out there and he turns up every morning to breakfast. Maybe he zips back in time and tucks them in every single night, a little millisecond late here or there from some tight spot; different face sometimes; they never mind.

Maybe he's their funny uncle. Maybe they are legion, woven across the sky; or maybe he has peered into every dark corner of the universe and decided he could never be so cruel as to bring an innocent life into it.

Who knows, maybe some of them are mine.

Although you'd think he'd have mentioned it.

Outside, there was a small knot of disgruntled park visitors – everyone else had gone home, but they were still there, clamouring for compensation and calling it disgusting. Amongst them was the large lady, with little Mure, who was sitting on the ground, crying and wailing in utter exhaustion, ignored by his mum, who was shouting about her rights.

'River,' said the Doctor. 'Give me your sword.'

'No,' I said. 'I like it and I want to keep it.'

'Give it to me.'

I grudgingly handed it over, and he took off all but a tiny rounded nub at the end with the sonic. Then he programmed something into it and handed it back to the child. Now, the blunt-edged sword played its own fireworks. He gave it to Mure, who stopped crying and we headed on back to the gates.

'I'm just saying, I liked that sword,' I said.

'Sssh,' said the Doctor.

We got to the edge of the Rainbow Bridge. Everyone had finally left; we had the entire park to ourselves. The Doctor winked at something that must have been a camera, and suddenly, the night lifted entirely, and suddenly we were in a perfect, golden dawn, in a meadow, next to the empty bridge, wildflowers everywhere and the warm sun on our necks.

'Picnic?'

*

After we'd eaten, he lay back, sighing in contentment, his head in my lap, and started pointing out the inconsistencies in the sky system. I could have mentioned that he was criticising a replica of a wholly imaginary atmosphere, but I don't think he'd have cared.

Then he stopped in mid-flow and reached up, one of his fingers – they seem, through every iteration, to stay abnormally long; Time Lord fingers are always a dead giveaway – twirling up through the curls in my hair.

'What are you thinking about?' he said. 'You look sad. I hate sad. It makes me itchy.'

I looked down at him. 'I know,' I said, and I stroked his cheek. 'It's nothing.'

'But you should still tell me, River-Runs-Deep. Shouldn't you? Should you? Is this one of those things I always get wrong, like flowers are GOOD presents and trees are NOT GOOD presents? Mystery of the Universe right there.'

'Mystery of the Universe,' I said, breathing out and trying to let go of the idea of that extraordinary thing I yearned for; life that remakes life on and on and on.

That no matter what the science tells you, the fact that something alive can grow inside you, something brand new and unique – even though it is made of the same mix of stardust and honey and hope as everything else that ever lived – is a mystery; that every baby is a piece of magic.

'You don't believe in magic, do you?' I said, and he laughed.

'No!'

I shoved him off then and jumped up. 'Well, that's a shame, because the Great Wiagler is doing a private show for us in five minutes, if you wanted to catch it.'

'Ooh! I do!' he said, scrambling to his feet. We started off in the direction of the beehive meridians.

'Does he shoot fiery breaths across the sky?'

'He shoots fiery breaths across the sky.'

'Does he juggle dragon eggs?'

'Yes, but they're very ethically sourced.'

'Will he let me choose the cards? Because, I have a system, right…'

And we did have fun. It was brilliant. We laughed and ate far too much, and he didn't even moan too much about the food, and we stayed up too late and I danced with Postumus on his new legs at the woodland staff celebration party under the three sickle moons and the Northern lights; and he got me back last night just before they sounded the alarms, and I lay on my cold stone bunk alone and thought what a fun family day out Asgard™ might make or could have made or was, one day.

They say a psychopath cannot imagine the world any other way but their own. That their version of reality is the only one that matters to them.

They are so wrong about me.

Suspicious Minds
Jacqueline Rayner

I first met Elvis in the Seventies. Of course, he was in disguise – no one was supposed to recognise him, that might have caused a riot. But I spotted him easily enough. I could tell at first glance he wasn't just one of the crowd, and it intrigued me. I determined then and there that I'd get him to myself, somehow or other.

I had to wait until the museum was closed for the night, but once the last cleaner had packed up her mop and bucket I simply put down my tray of oranges (oh yes – I'd swapped places with a wax Nell Gwynn; we share a taste for tumbling curls, and boned bodices and scooped necklines have always been my friends), walked over to his section and simply leaned, arms crossed, by a model of Elton John and stared at him.

I'll give Elvis his due, he managed to stare back for over an hour before he blinked. But then I knew I had him.

'What's a nice Auton like you doing in a place like this?' I asked.

'Ah'm just hangin',' he said in a Southern drawl that sounded enticingly exotic in the London of Three-Day Weeks, National Front marches and bombing campaigns by the IRA. Honestly, it was a bleak time to visit. I'd only decided to drop in because I'd heard that no fewer than three separate incarnations of Himself got together round about now and I had a huge desire to have a look at what a car crash that would be. It turned out to be really disappointing, though; most of it happened in an antimatter universe so I missed all that, and Grandpa Grouch (I haven't yet come across one of him I haven't liked the look of, but goodness he seems to have been really grumpy back in the day) barely turned up at all. If it hadn't been for meeting Elvis I'd have considered the whole thing a washout.

We chatted through the night. Well, not just chatting. But the chatting was fun too. He'd been 'just hangin'' for a while, since a botched recent Nestene invasion attempt and – small universe alert! – it was only a certain non-medical man of my close acquaintance who'd foiled the aliens' plan! We laughed a lot about that. Most of Elvis's fellow Autons had been deactivated when the Nestene Consciousness left Earth, but somehow he'd managed to retain his sentience, perhaps – and this is just my theory – because he so desperately wanted to. Just that short time on Earth between invasion and thwarting had turned him into a fully fledged humanophile. Unfortunately for him he wasn't one of the really accurate replicas who could pass as human so he'd been forced to stay in the one place where no one would spot him – Madame Tussauds. Originally, as part of the slightly complicated Nestene plan, he'd been some obscure politician, but when that exhibition was closed down he'd tried on various heads until finally settling on Elvis Presley. I think it was the sequins that swayed him. Plus the fact that no one was likely to be melting Elvis down any time soon.

Elvis loved people-watching but he was clearly grateful for slightly more personal interaction, and I'd had a good time too so it wasn't too much of a hardship to agree to pop back and visit him every now and again. Admittedly I only managed it every decade or so, but we made the most of each opportunity. He was pretty much always Elvis, apart from a brief spell in the Eighties when he tried out Jason Donovan, and after the sad events of August 1977 we sometimes even ventured out in public (at night, when his plasticness didn't show as much) as there was no danger of anyone mistaking him for the real King of Rock and Roll. Well, I say that – blurry 'Elvis is alive!' pictures did turn up in the more sensationalist newspapers, but most people assumed they were about as real as the Patterson-Gimlin Bigfoot film. (Not me: I knew Elvis was dead but Bigfoot was definitely real. We'd hung out a few times. Her name was Geraldine and she was really annoyed that the film-makers caught her on a bad hair day.)

Elvis and I painted the town red a couple of times in the Eighties and Nineties and all was going swimmingly until one day in the mid 2000s. I'd entered the museum with a party of Bulgarian tourists and given the King a little wave as we passed by so he'd know tonight was the night, then I'd slipped into the farthingale and ruff of Good Queen Bess (I was gradually working my way through the curly-haired of history) to wait for closing time.

And then *he* turned up. Fez and bow tie and tweed jacket. (Some of the visitors thought he was an interactive exhibit; I overheard them trying to work out who he was meant to be.) Well, I couldn't resist. I waited until he was within touching distance then I leaned forward and whispered, 'Hello, Sweetie.'

He jumped a mile then tried to pretend he hadn't, a great bundle of long arms and legs like a startled flamingo. Then he looked at me and wagged a bony finger in my face. 'Oh no no no. No no no. That is not on.'

'What isn't?' I asked, giving a twirl (the Bulgarian tourists started applauding).

'Wife dressing up as previous wife. That's just…' He started to grin, so I gave him a hard stare.

'Is this guy bothering you?' Oh dear. That was Elvis, swaggering over to us. The Bulgarians applauded again. The Doctor looked him up and down then whipped out his sonic.

'River, run!'

'What, in these skirts?'

'It's an Auton! I'll hold it off while you… shuffle slowly away.'

I rolled my eyes and put a hand on Elvis's arm. 'Doctor, Elvis the Auton, Elvis the Auton, Doctor. All friends here.'

The Doctor looked scandalised. 'Friends? With a plastic-brained drudge of the Nestene Consciousness?'

'Who are you callin' plastic-brained?'

I put a hand on each's chest and pushed them apart before fists could be raised. 'Boys, boys. This isn't the time or the place.' (I didn't have a more appropriate time or place in mind, I just felt like doing my 'teacher' voice.) 'Doctor, what are you doing here?'

He looked sheepish and began to fiddle with his bow tie. No answer was forthcoming, but I could read his face like a book. I tried not to grin but I just couldn't help it; I could feel a big smile spreading across my face. 'This is another of your ways of keeping score, isn't it? You pop in, check out who're the current crop of celebrities then engineer meetings with those you haven't come across before so you'll be able to sprinkle their names in conversation. Madame Tussauds is basically your personal namedropping checklist.'

More bow tie fiddling.

'Elvis, what are the latest models?'

The Auton thought for a few seconds. 'Few months ago we got Posh and Becks – oh, and the Andrex puppy.'

'There you go, Doctor. You'd better go and look up the Andrex puppy. Take it for walkies. Everyone will be so impressed.'

'Better the Andrex puppy than a… a… *hound dog*.'

'Don't be cruel,' I told him. 'Elvis was just a lonely man.'

'He's the Devil in disguise!'

'You have such a suspicious mind.'

'And you're a hard-headed women with a wooden heart who's got me all shook up!'

I sighed. 'Any minute now you're going to accuse me of stepping on your blue suede shoes. Look, this is all great fun, but maybe we should talk about it somewhere less public…?'

The Bulgarian tourists were entranced by our performance. As we shuffled out of the gallery, a couple came forward to press ten-leva notes into our hands. One man even tried to shove a fistful of notes down my bodice, which the Doctor retrieved and gave back to him with an icy 'return to sender'.

We found a quiet spot in the Chamber of Horrors, and I dragged the Doctor into a gaol cell (admittedly, that felt a bit close to home) while Elvis perched on a guillotine a little way away.

'Look, Elvis is a good guy. You'd like him if you got to know him.'

'How many times has that sentence been said in the history of the universe?'

I shrugged. 'Doesn't mean it isn't true.'

'River, listen to me. Stay away from him.'

Well, that didn't go down very well. How long has he known me? (That's not a rhetorical question, by the way. We haven't established where this encounter fits in our timelines yet.) However long it is, though, he surely knew within minutes of our first meeting that he has no say in who I associate with. Even if he thinks he's acting for my own good.

Hang on, though. There was a clue to how long he'd known me. 'You called me your wife!' I said.

His eyes went wide. (I love his eyes. Green, the colour of mystery. They're youthful and ancient at the same time, and oh, I could look into them for hours. Days. Decades.) 'Am I, er, being a bit presumptuous…? And, er, totally unrelated, do you happen to have your diary on you…?'

I chuckled. 'It's all right, I think we're on the same page. I just meant, you called me your wife. So, for you – as well as for me – that's already happened.'

He visibly relaxed.

I continued. 'And that being so, it also means that you are well aware that there can be "good" Autons. My father, for example.'

'Are you supposed to be able to remember that?' he asked.

'I'm not sure if I'm *supposed* to,' I said with a shrug. 'But I do. And you're ignoring my point.'

'River,' he said. 'Listen carefully to me.'

'Oh, I thought I'd just tune in for one word in three,' I said, smiling but inwardly slightly irritated. I always listen carefully to him. Always. Might not agree with what I'm listening to, might not act on it, but he will never not have my full attention.

'I'm not trying to patronise you,' he said. 'I'm not playing the jealous husband. But I know something that you probably don't know. In a few weeks' time, the Nestenes will launch another invasion attempt. I can't do anything about that, because I've already done something about it, and I get very annoyed with myself if I try to interfere with what I'm doing.'

'So?'

'So, your buddy Elvis here is going to find himself dragged back into the fold. Oh, he might have been able to ride out a minor invasion or two in the past, ones where the Nestenes didn't get that far, but not this one. This is a biggie. He won't be able to keep his autonomy, no joke intended, no really, River, take that look off your face. He'll become a danger to you. Rory – he was a different story. He had a very strong personality to build on in the first place, and he had a powerful motivation. The rules didn't apply to him. But they will to Mr Jailhouse Rock.'

And it would be like a death. Elvis would have left the building.

'I'll have to tell him,' I said, saddened.

So there, in the chamber of horrors, surrounded by instruments of torture and the images of death-bringers, I explained to Elvis that his life would soon be over.

A plastic face doesn't really show emotions. Or so I'd thought until now.

'Yeah, I kinda guessed that would happen some day,' he said. 'My old buddies the Nestenes think this planet is a mighty fine place. I just thought I'd keep on hiding just like I been doin'.'

'I don't think you'll be able to,' said the Doctor, kindly now. 'I'm sorry.'

'There is one thing…' I looked from the Doctor to Elvis and back again. 'We could…' I held the Doctor's gaze. 'Couldn't we?'

He didn't have to ask what I was trying to say. 'I… could. If it means that much to you.'

Elvis doesn't share our gift of matrimonial telepathy, though. And he did have a plastic brain. He still looked clueless.

'The Doctor can take you away from here,' I explained. 'Keep you out of range.'

My Auton friend shook his head. 'Nu-huh,' he said. 'Thank you kindly, but this is my home. This time, this place, this planet.'

'I could bring you back, after the invasion's over,' said the Doctor.

'And then I just sit here waiting for the next time? No.' He pulled himself up to Elvis's full six feet. 'I won't leave – but I won't turn into a killing machine again. Tell me the date they arrive, Doctor. I'll deactivate myself before then.'

'You can't—' I began.

He chose to take me literally. 'I can. There's a big ol' furnace down in the basement.'

I shuddered, imagining those well-loved features melting away.

'You have fourteen days,' said the Doctor. I could see he was itching to get away from here. Oh, big dramatic scenes don't bother him, but little dramas like this make him very uncomfortable. A huge passionate speech on the fate of the universe? Fine. The look on the face of a creature that's going to melt itself down in a fortnight? Awkward. But I wasn't going to leave it like this.

'One last hurrah,' I suggested. 'See the world before… well. Before. Is there somewhere you'd like to go?'

There were several answers he might have given that wouldn't have surprised me at all. Graceland, obviously. (Viva) Las Vegas. (Blue) Hawaii. Maybe even the bright lights of Blackpool. But no. I was slightly bemused to hear him ask, 'You heard of the meadows?'

'Any meadows in particular?' said the Doctor. 'The Candle Meadows of Karass Don Slava? Grantchester Meadows? The Meadows Shopping Centre, Chelmsford?'

Elvis shook his head. 'No, sir. I guess they're just called "the meadows". Heard some visitors talking about them. Most beautiful place on Earth they said, only they said it was pretty exclusive. I sure would like to see the most beautiful place on Earth, although I guess – well, that might not be possible. Bit too difficult, seeing as I don't even know where they are.'

Well, hinting that something might not be possible or is too difficult is the surest way I know of getting the Doctor to want to give it a go. He hurried out of the room, apologising to a wax model of George Joseph Smith that he bumped into on the way, and returned within minutes to announce that he'd located it, found out what it was, and – ta da! – had got us all visiting permits.

I took the passes he held out. 'Dr John Smith, Dr River Smith and Dr Elvis Smith of the International Dung Beetle Alliance?'

'Er, yes.'

'*Dung Beetle* Alliance?'

'Don't you go knocking the dung beetle. I'll have you know that *Onthophagus taurus* can pull 1,141 times its own bodyweight.'

That wasn't really an explanation. As I pointed out.

'Well. This meadows place is all about insects, so I thought if I made us all about insects they'd be more likely to let us in. Our coprophagiac friends happened to be the first ones that sprang to mind. Here, have a pamphlet.'

I took the pamphlet. I read the pamphlet. The Doctor was right, it was all about insects. In fact, it was close to a rant about insects. About their importance, and their decline, and how man was a wicked, wicked species to allow it to happen. I felt quite guilty on behalf of the whole of humankind after reading it, and tried to work out how many times in my life I'd swatted a fly. Too many for comfort, I think. But I agreed to take a trip to this insect paradise with my boys.

Even having visited them, I still don't know exactly where the meadows are. Somewhere in the Mediterranean, I'd say, from the colour of the sky – oh, hark at me. I'm starting to sound like a certain Mr 'just dip a finger in the water and lick it and pretend you can tell exact latitude and longitude by its salt content' (and I know for a fact that he only pulls that stunt when he's just had a sneaky look at some TARDIS monitor or other).

But anyway, we arrived at wherever it was, and the sun shone, and the sky was clear, and the air was sweet, and the whole place was surrounded by a force barrier. That was rather a surprise, as it seemed a bit advanced for this time period. I suggested this might indicate alien involvement so we'd better tread carefully, but the Doctor assured me (correctly, as it turned out) that the technology was available on Earth at this time, for those with the money, the contacts and the necessary obsession. It was quite clear from the moment we met Melissa that she had the latter in spades.

Melissa Tokana was short and blonde, and it was hard to tell her age. Not that that's particularly suspicious. I mean, look at the three of us. I'm not entirely sure how old I am, for a start. Then there's the Doctor, who's 1,000-plus and looks barely a day over 30, and Elvis, who looks – and is – 30-ish, but has done so since he was about a week old.

Melissa met us – and the other visitors, ones who'd arrived by more conventional means than Gallifreyan time ship – in person, and welcomed us to her world.

'Why the force field?' I asked her. 'To stop the flies flying off?'

'Indeed,' she said – to my surprise, as I was being slightly facetious; obviously I'd assumed it was to keep unwelcome visitors out. 'What use would it be to nurture them here then allow them into a world that is slowly destroying their kind?'

'So the purpose of this place is just conservation?' I said. 'You're not trying to change the world?'

'Oh, but I am. And when man wakes up to the damage being done to the Earth, my insects and I will be here. Ready.'

Yeah, good luck with that. I'm from the fifty-first century, and I can tell you humankind's never going to wake up to the damage it's doing. It just does it, says 'Oops!', then does it again.

We were taken through the force field into a building that resembled a beehive, a honeycombed structure that disoriented you immediately. Doors led off in all directions, and although many of the partitions were made of glass, the refraction of sunlight and the warped views through created a maze effect, a hall of mirrors that left you not quite knowing if you were going up, down or sideways. Melissa led us into a hexagonal room that had several aspects to the outside, but all I could make out for sure was that everywhere outside was just… green. Endless greenery isn't entirely my cup of tea, but we were doing this for Elvis, not me – and anyway, it would probably be more appealing when seen in full rather than glimpsed through a distorting lens.

It didn't look like we were going to get to the great outdoors for a while, though. Apparently we first had to listen to a talk on being nice to gnats – or something like that – before Melissa decided we were worthy of viewing her precious meadows. I suppose I couldn't really blame her. This was her life's work, a haven for insects, a painstaking recreation of the ideal ecosystem for many species to flourish. She didn't want tourists trampling all over the place. (She was very unimpressed that the Doctor had brought a picnic hamper. He tried to hide it behind his back but she confiscated it anyway.) Resigned to our fate, we sat down to hear her pre-visit talk.

Melissa stood before us, her eyes glittering, and addressed the universe via the couple of dozen humans assembled in front of her. 'The insect. So small, so insignificant. Who would notice if the world had no more insects?'

It was obviously a rhetorical question, but the Doctor put up his hand anyway. 'I would!'

Melissa looked slightly surprised to have audience participation this soon into her talk, but gave him a pleased smile. 'Yes indeed. Insects may be tiny but their importance is enormous, in so many different areas.'

The Doctor put up his hand again. 'Ooh ooh ooh!'

Her smile was not quite so pleased this time. 'Yes?'

'For example, pollination.' The Doctor beamed at everyone around him. He does like being the star pupil.

She nodded. 'Pollination. Insects are essential for the pollination not only of decorative plants but of fruits and vegetables – a food source for both humans and animals.'

'Humans are animals,' the Doctor interjected, without putting his hand up.

It was just an aside. Of course, I knew he was referring to their taxonomical classification rather than being rude, but it's more fun pretending to take offence. 'Human wife sitting right next to you!' I pointed out.

'And would you deny, River, that you can sometimes be a bit of an animal?'

Ah, compliments will get you anywhere. I shot him a smile. Melissa, less impressed, waited impatiently for us to stop interrupting.

'Of course, insects themselves are also part of the food chain, an important source of food for many creatures – birds, reptiles, mammals and more – which are themselves part of the food chain for others. So without insects, both plant- and meat-eaters would find themselves going hungry. But the insects' role in food production goes even deeper than that.'

I could see resignation in her eyes as the Doctor put up his hand for a third time. She really hadn't intended this to be an interactive session.

'Yes?' said Melissa.

'Soil,' said the Doctor smugly.

'Yes. Soil. Would you like to elaborate?' The words came out between gritted teeth. But then the Doctor would try the patience even of teachers used to dealing with hyperactive 5-year-olds.

'Oh, no no no. You're the expert.'

'Thank you. Well—'

'And I'm sure you're going to talk about their role in aerating soil as well as in digesting animal dung.'

'I *was*, yes.'

'Good good good.' The Doctor sat back and folded his arms expectantly.

'Insects aerate the soil,' said Melissa. 'They also break up and digest animal dung.' She sighed. I could see the Doctor beginning to sit up again, and so could she because she started talking quickly. 'It's not just animal dung that they dispose of. Without them, the planet would drown under the weight of rotted matter, animal and vegetable. The slug, for example, is an essential tool in waste management, consuming rotting flesh and vegetation.'

'And my lettuces!' called out a gentleman from the audience. The woman sitting next to him giggled.

Melissa did not look amused. 'Insects are essential for life, and essential to deal with death,' she continued.

'And slug pellets are essential if you want to keep your cabbages!' said the same man.

The lecture dragged on. I had plastered a look of polite interest on my face but it threatened to slip every now and again as Melissa continued listing the many, many wonderful things about insects and humanity's terrible, terrible effect on their populations. One of the problems with fanatics is that their very passion can get your back up. I'd gone into the talk thinking that humanity really should take more care of its various six-legged, three-segmented little buddies, but after what felt like hours of Melissa's diatribe I was on the verge of indulging in a little light destruction of natural habitats with a side order of pesticides myself.

But not everyone was as fed up as me. I'd been looking between Melissa (ordinary human politeness) and the Doctor (fascination at what he might do next), and hadn't really spared a thought for Elvis the Auton (although I had noted earlier that everyone else was trying not to stare at him. You don't often come across walking, talking plastic Elvis replicas in day-to-day life). But now I heard a sort of sigh of admiration (impressive as he doesn't actually breathe; I happen to know he'd spent 1979 to 1980 perfecting human vocal mannerisms). I turned to him and saw a visionary look in his solid plastic eyes. He was buying every syllable she uttered.

'Ma'am,' he said. 'If I'm understanding you right, you're sayin' that humanity couldn't survive without insects?'

'That's it in a nutshell, Dr Smith. And yet everything needed for insect life is being taken away. Forests cut down, hedgerows destroyed. Bogs drained. Roads and houses built on irreplaceable insect habitats.'

A woman in oversized sunglasses leant forward. 'I wonder if you're not being a little bit naïve,' she said. 'No offence meant.'

Well, offence had clearly been taken, as I could see from Melissa's expression. But the woman ignored it and carried on anyway.

'Progress has got to be made. I understand exactly what you're saying, and I'm all for preservation of wildlife. But I'm also for housing, road-building and high agricultural yield. I think a compromise is possible.'

I didn't think that Melissa was the sort of person who compromised.

The sunglasses woman waved a hand and smiled. 'What you're doing here is great. But in the end it's not going to change the world. It's just an insect zoo.'

'No! She's saving mankind!' Well, that was a surprise. Elvis had jumped to his feet, a devoted new disciple if ever I saw one. 'Don't you understand? Humans can't live without insects. In saving these insects here, this gal is saving the human race! Saving humans from themselves! Giving them back the home that man has taken away.'

Oh, Melissa liked that. She beamed at Elvis. 'Yes! My meadows are a recreation of the perfect ecosystem for many important species. Out there you will find varieties of butterflies and moths, grasshoppers and crickets, dragonflies and damsel flies – bees, of course – glow-worms, beetles… It would take me hours to list them all.'

I took a deep breath. It didn't seem impossible that she would decide to do that. What's another hour or two listing insect species among friends? To my relief, though, she didn't.

I'd probably been aware of the buzzing noise for a while before I consciously realised it was there. Barely audible, really, and my brain had been off on its own trying to distract itself from Melissa's rant. Even when I had noticed the sound, I didn't think a lot of it. Wasps don't bother me (I once spent a lovely weekend with a Vespiform called Roderick) and we were, after all, basically on the doorstep of an Insect Shangri-La. Having the creature buzzing around the room was a tiny bit irritating, but so what?

And then a man swatted it. A real, full-on *whack* with a book. No possible escape. Insect pancake.

Well, Melissa didn't say anything, but her eyebrows jumped to the sky. If she'd had a giant-size book on her, I wouldn't have been at all surprised if the wasp-splatter got splatted in turn. I was tensed, ready for action.

But nothing happened. Melissa's face returned to normal, and I relaxed. Well, maybe I kept myself very slightly on alert (my suspicious mind at work again). That would be why I noticed what I noticed later on.

The talk finally neared its end. I was feeling very sorry for Elvis. Only fourteen days to live, and he'd had to use a few of his precious final hours (OK, actually minutes; it just felt like hours) listening to a small fierce human lecture us about woodlice. But he didn't seem to think it had been a waste. In fact, when Melissa came to her impassioned conclusion – 'Do you agree? Do you agree that insect life must be preserved at any cost?!' – Elvis jumped to his feet and whooped 'Hallelujah! The insects must live, for the glory of the human race!' (The Doctor and I – and most of the other audience members – opted for slightly more low-key agreements.)

Well, after that, we were finally deemed worthy of entry into the meadows. We were divided into small groups of three or four to be sent off in different directions, with a request not to stray from our allotted segment. Melissa very plausibly explained that too many people in one place could prove dangerous to the fragile ecosystems she'd so painstakingly encouraged. Yes, that was very plausible. Not suspicious at all. Except I happened to notice that one of her groups consisted of the man who wasn't keen on slugs, the woman with him (his wife?) who'd laughed at his remarks, the man who'd killed the wasp, and the woman in sunglasses who was keen on roads and houses and crops. I casually wandered nearer as Melissa spoke with them.

'Now then, you'll have gathered I'm a bit of a gardener,' said the slug man – short, red-faced, big moustache – 'and it amazes me how well these meadows of yours grow, just left to themselves.'

'Oh, they're not left entirely to themselves,' said Melissa. 'There's the 206.'

'And what's that?' asked the man. 'A planting protocol?'

'A fertiliser,' she replied. 'Possibly the best fertiliser there is.'

The red-faced man's eyes lit up. 'Now I am very interested in fertilisers,' he said. 'I'm guessing you go for the organic types. What is this 206? Compost? Manure? Blood or bone meal?'

'It's my own very special blend,' said Melissa.

'And you couldn't give a fellow gardener a clue about your secret recipe?'

'Well, perhaps,' said Melissa. 'Perhaps I could give you a hint. As you're a fellow gardener.'

I was watching her face. She was smiling, there was no hint of the – well, annoyance was probably too mild a word – that had crossed her features after the unfortunate wasp-splatting incident. But there was something in her expression… something familiar… something worrying.

It was on the tip of my mind, but I couldn't reach it.

'River!' The Doctor was calling me. He'd been restless throughout the talk, now he couldn't wait to be on the move again. I put the mystery of Melissa's expression out of my mind as I rejoined the Doctor and Elvis – our own little group – and waited to be allowed out.

Melissa went around letting the groups out one at a time. We didn't just walk out of a door into the meadows, we made our disorientated way through more honeycomb passages until an exit opened before us. I looked around as we went out, hoping to see where the slug and sunglasses group had got to, but there were no other humans in sight.

To be honest, I was so overwhelmed by what greeted us that the other groups faded from my mind almost at once. Did I say that green wasn't really my scene? Well, maybe not, but 'green' was only a description of this kaleidoscope of varying shades in the same way that 'a bunch of notes' is a description of Beethoven's Pastoral Symphony. And it wasn't as if green was all there was, either. The plains ahead had rainbows sprinkled through them. Red poppies to orange hawkweed, yellow cowslip, green nettles with tiny white flowers, the brilliant blue of cornflowers blending into indigo vetch and pretty violet scabious. It felt so peaceful that you assumed it was quiet too, until you concentrated and realised that there was a constant underlying hum of a million insects. The chirrup of crickets, the friendly buzz of bees. Grasses high enough to tickle my chin; little woven nests in the grass with tiny brown mouse noses poking out. Birds swooping, perching, whistling. Rabbits skittered by, unafraid, and a grass snake slid over Elvis's shoe, to his utter delight.

And so many perfumes, so many different scents weaved together to create such sweetness. If it could be bottled it'd be worth a fortune. *'Meadows' by Calvin Klein.*

Elvis had chosen well. This was a place that would bring peace and tranquillity to his final days. We walked on together, the three of us, not speaking, deeper and deeper into the wilderness, our senses overwhelmed by the beauty around us, wishing there were more places like this in the world. Oh, humanity. Was there ever a gift given to you that you did not break? I am one of you but I am also a child of time and I have witnessed so much. Knowing myself as I do, I don't presume to lecture you on war or hatred, but I wish you'd take more care of the little things: the birds and the bees and the flowers. Beauty is precious.

Oh, and as Melissa pointed out, also incredible necessary for, you know, the continuation of life on Earth.

Such a short time in these meadows and I was already a convert. Suddenly all that humourless ranting seemed fully justified. I understood why Melissa and that woman who preferred roads to grasshoppers could never be friends.

I like to dress appropriately for my surroundings and I'd changed earlier in the TARDIS; now I did my best impression of a romantic heroine as I walked barefoot through the grass, white skirts swishing around my ankles. I knew that both my romantic heroes were looking on in appreciation, but I wasn't doing it for them. I unpinned the visitor's pass from my chest; it didn't go with the look. 'Dr River Smith', indeed.

And then I froze.

Smith.

The wasp-killer, the woman who liked houses. The man who used slug pellets. I suddenly knew where I'd seen Melissa's expression before, that queer triumphant smile. That was the expression worn by the waxwork of George Joseph Smith, the one the Doctor had tripped over back in Madame Tussauds Chamber of Horrors. Smith, the man who persuaded his wives to insure their lives and make wills in his favour and then drowned them in their baths. Yes, I was sure of it. His arrogant smile – the one that said, 'You are encompassing your own destruction at my command' – had been reproduced line for line on Melissa's face. My previous suspicions jumped to the forefront of my mind again.

The Doctor had found a spot where the grass was short and soft, and was sitting cross-legged on the ground, blowing at a dandelion clock. 'Three o'clock!' he announced. 'Time for a picnic.'

'I thought Melissa confiscated your picnic,' I said.

He produced a rather squashed jam sandwich from his pocket, followed by a thermos flask that couldn't possibly have fitted in there. 'Ah, she may have confiscated my picnic *hamper*, but I managed to liberate some of the picnic itself. Sandwich? Fizzy pop?'

I politely declined. I know what else he keeps in his pockets.

Now, the Doctor has a finely tuned evil-detector located slap bang in the centre of his very big brain. If he hadn't sensed anything 'off' about Melissa, then there wasn't likely to be anything to sense. And he looked so happy sprawled on the grass in this perfect place. Elvis did too. I didn't want to ruin that, for either of them, but especially for the one who was going to die soon. The trouble was, that brides-in-the-bath expression was haunting me.

'I'm going to walk a bit further,' I said. 'Build up an appetite.'

The Doctor tossed across his sonic. 'Setting 674 alpha 2,' he said. 'Compass.'

That wasn't a bad idea. I have a wonderful sense of direction, but this place was vast and wild. I tucked it into my waistband.

I thought back to the way we'd come and tried to calculate the direction I'd need to walk in to intercept the next party. I turned and headed that way. But I was in for a shock – literally. I'd walked maybe half a mile when I slammed into an invisible wall, electricity juddering through me. There, right in the middle of the meadows, was another force field.

Well, that hadn't been mentioned. Perhaps it was just a way of keeping us from straying too far. Or perhaps it was something more sinister.

I walked first one way then the other in an attempt to see how far the barrier stretched, but there was no end in sight. I was half tempted to just go back to the Doctor and Elvis, ridiculing my own silly suspicions, but I'm stubborn and I wanted to know what was going on. And I had a sonic screwdriver with me! Didn't take me long to figure out how to disable the barrier.

'Hello?' I called as I walked on, but no one replied. I kept going.

As I wandered I found that the perfume of the flowers and the buzzing of the insects became almost hypnotic, each of my senses soothed in turn.

My life – well, my life hasn't known much calm, and that's the way I like it. Being thrown from one death-defying escapade to the next is what keeps me going. Oh, occasionally I've dabbled in deliberately peaceful activities like yoga (being able to put your legs behind your head helps in so many areas of life), meditation or those adult colouring books that bizarrely became a craze in AD 2015, but I prefer action. It stops me from thinking. Thinking about what I've done, or what I am. Or what I wish would turn out differently but know it never can.

The peace here was so engrossing though that it kept even the smallest melancholy thought at bay. Perhaps I had found the one place in the universe where I could be truly content. Finding the other people didn't seem important any more. I'd been over-reacting. Nothing bad could happen in a place like this.

I sank to the ground and began to make a chain of ox-eye daisies. When I'd linked enough I turned it into a circlet for my hair; a more perfect crown than any of Queen Elizabeth's rubies or pearls.

Thinking of my conjugal predecessor made me think of the Doctor. Oh, who am I trying to fool? *Everything* makes me think of the Doctor. I'm not exactly jealous he had a life before me – or after me – or during me (time travel is so complicated) – and my life has hardly been a wilderness outside of him. But I'm sometimes scared at how much of my well-being is tied up with that man. He hovers above my consciousness continually. He'd be horrified if he knew that – but then, I think he does know, really.

I should have known things were wrong when I first began to forget about him.

Not in a crack-in-the-universe way, not like he was wiped from my mind, but like he didn't matter any more. The Doctor not mattering to me was something I'd never experienced before.

And yet I didn't care.

I could feel him draining from my mind, and I had no desire to hold on, to make a grab for him, to pull him back to me.

Without the Doctor, maybe I could at last welcome peace.

I trailed my hands through the flowers, disturbing a jewel-like dragonfly. The scent of apples wafted up from a clump of camomile, and pollen speckled my skin. My daisy circlet tumbled from my hair as I lay my head on a pillow of cowslips and ragged robin.

So much calm.

So much contentment.

So much peace.

NO!

I struggled, just for a moment. I wouldn't let the Doctor slip from my mind entirely. Oh, maybe I could never welcome peace while he was a part of me. But I knew for certain I would never welcome peace without him.

I reached out, flailing like a baby, grasping desperately for him. He would always be there to catch me as I fall…

My fingers clasped his hand and I was filled with relief.

Except…

His fingers were bony, but not *that* bony.

I fought harder against the all-consuming calm, desperately struggling to reach the surface again. I whispered his name under my breath, over and over, a mantra to keep me afloat. I hadn't realised my eyes were shut until I discovered how hard it was to open them. It would be so easy just to give in…

Just sleep.

Just peace.

For ever.

My eyes snapped open. I stared at the thing I was holding. A hand of bone in my hand of flesh. More bones leading away from it, still attached, arm bones that folded in on themselves, clattering to the ground as I hurriedly let go of the hand.

Still desperately trying not to give in to sleep – a rest that I now realised would be eternal – I crawled through the long grass. As it parted with my progress I came on more bones – not scattered ones, not random, as with the first these still had scraps of leathery sinew holding them together. Once-human forms. Some gleaming white, some still shrouded in black masses of beetles and other insects.

Perhaps I should have tried to get back to the Doctor and Elvis, but I was hardly thinking clearly. My head was swimming but I forced myself onwards, because I knew now the fate that was awaiting those four people who hadn't shared Melissa's dream of an insect-filled world.

My white skirts became green with grass stains as I forced myself to keep going. Standing up was beyond me still, and sometimes I could see where I was going and sometimes, if the grass was too high, I could not. On and on. Hand and knee forward, hand and knee forward, keep to the rhythm and you can do it. I was sleepwalking – no, sleepcrawling – but I was still in control. Just.

I found the woman in sunglasses first. One arm of the sunglasses was still over an ear, the other bent wildly out of shape, perhaps twisted as she lay down. I couldn't tell if she was still breathing; I bent my head down to listen and the heaviness and weariness overtook me again. I lay by her side, close, just about feeling the tiniest rise and fall of her chest. She was alive, but I couldn't move. I didn't want to. The peace had pulled me back in and added something new: I was a child clutched to the bosom of her mother, hearing a mother's gentle breathing, a sound that said 'I will protect you always. I will keep you safe. You just have to stay with me.'

Oh, how deeply I felt that right then! But the thing is, I also knew it was a lie. I'd never been that child. My mother had never clasped me to her. Oh, she'd wanted to, I know that, this wasn't about blame or even about pity for myself. It was just about reality. And reality gave me a crutch to lean on.

I pushed the peace out of my mind and replaced it with anger. Anger at being taken from my parents. Anger at the life stolen from me. Anger at the people who'd made me what I am. (I'd like to say 'what I was'. But I can never be entirely sure.) Anger at a universe that allowed this to happen. Perhaps, even, anger at the Doctor, because loving him might make life so much better, but it made it oh, so much harder too.

Sustained by anger, I managed to get to my feet. I stumbled forwards and found the other three. All unconscious, all barely alive. I wanted to help, but how?

The air was heavier here. The sweet scent I'd noted earlier had transformed into something sickly and cloying. Every time I breathed in, a wave of drowsiness hit me. It was something in the air that was causing this soporific state. I tried, fruitlessly, to drag the unconscious bodies away, but the air was sapping my strength and the more I tried, the more sleep threatened to overwhelm me again. I had to leave them behind to fetch help.

What I needed was someone who didn't breathe. And by a stroke of luck, I knew exactly where I could find such a person.

Well, almost exactly. I staggered round in circles for a few minutes, before remembering why the Doctor had given me the sonic screwdriver in the first place. In my dazed and confused state, I don't think I'd have made it back to them without it.

There were more bones underfoot on the way back. I'm not the sentimental type, but perhaps it was the dreamlike state I couldn't quite escape from that made me imagine how they'd once looked clothed in flesh. Those bones had worn faces that smiled and frowned, faces that had meant so much to parents, children, lovers. Time, and death, and Melissa, had stolen those faces from them.

After a while, there were no more bones. I was back in my original segment of the meadows. The sickening scent still hung in the air but it was lighter now and I found it easier to walk. I was even able to summon the energy to call out. 'Doctor! Doctor!'

No one called back, but then I saw Elvis, in the distance, waving at me. I struggled on. As I approached, he put a finger to his lips. 'The Doctor's having a little ol' nap,' he whispered as I got close enough to hear. 'Guess saving the universe all the time is a pretty tiring business.'

'NO!' I wasn't sure if I'd shouted aloud or in my head until I saw Elvis's shocked expression. There was the Doctor, still sprawled on the ground where I'd left him, a smile of utter peace and contentment on his face. I flung myself down beside him and shook him hard. 'Wake up, Doctor! Wake up!'

His eyes flickered open and his smile grew wider, but he was barely focusing. 'River? What have I told you about sneaking into my bedroom at night?'

'It's not night time and this isn't your bedroom,' I told him firmly. 'And I need you to wake up. Now!'

The urgency in my voice penetrated at last and he pushed himself up on to his elbows. 'Whassup?' he said, still sleepy but more himself.

'Melissa's drugging people and turning them into fertiliser,' I told him. I was working it out in my head as I explained it to him. 'The people who share her vision get all this inner peace and calm and then when they leave the meadows they spread the word, about how beautiful it all is, and how conservation is so essential, all that stuff. But she weeds out those who aren't going to fall in with her plans, separates them from the others and gives them the sort of peace that has "rest in" in front of it.'

'Tha's ver' int'restin…' slurred the Doctor, lying back down again and closing his eyes. I shook him really hard this time.

'You will not go back to sleep! Look, this is my fault. I took down the force barrier and the gas, or whatever it is, is spreading wider afield. But you're a Time Lord! Switch on your respiratory bypass system or something! There are people to save!'

That's the sort of clarion call he always responds to. In seconds he was sitting up, shaking his head as if to expel the gas from it, and looking at me with eyes now fully alert. 'That's not exactly how the respiratory bypass system works,' he said. 'But good call, Gallifreyan physiology, that'll keep me safe for a bit.'

We set off. Elvis was not happy. His illusions had been shattered. I saw his face and he didn't look angry, more like a puppy that couldn't understand why his beloved master was kicking him. 'But she was doing it to help the humans,' he said, sad and puzzled. 'Why would she kill them?'

Well, the answer to that was pretty clear. I've met enough 'greater good' types in my life. But I wasn't sure I could adequately explain these complexities to Elvis, who was a simple soul at (plastic – not wooden) heart.

I was wearing Elvis's satin scarf tied over my mouth and nose as a makeshift gasmask and the Doctor had shown me some breathing techniques that would minimise the amount I inhaled. Neither were fully effective, but it meant I should be able to keep going a bit longer so I could find Melissa's victims.

I could tell we were getting close to the place as the gas began to get heavier and my steps began to slow down. You know when you try to run in dreams but find you can barely move, your legs weighed down in treacle? It was like that, but for real. At least we had Elvis with us so if either the Doctor or I did succumb, he'd be there to wake us up. And then I knew we were definitely in the right place because we started to trip over bones again.

'Worm food,' said the Doctor, looking down at yet another corpse. Which is when I realised the full horror of the situation.

Melissa had said that she owed the success of the meadows to the 206 – her very special fertiliser. And I'd just realised what that was.

There are 206 bones in the human body. Bone meal is one of the most nutritious types of fertiliser. Melissa wasn't just killing the people who didn't share her vision, she was building her insect empire on the bones of her enemies, feeding them to the soil, growing the meadows that her insects needed to survive. The circle of life, created by death.

I led the Doctor and Elvis to the four unconscious dissenters and Elvis, slightly helped but probably more hindered by the Doctor and me, carried them out of the danger zone. Then the Doctor got out the sonic screwdriver (I'd given it back, of course) and zipped and zapped to restore the force field, so the gas would stop escaping. Except he couldn't.

'You popped it like a bubble,' he said. 'Can't restore a bubble from the pop.'

'Well, can you blow a new bubble, then?' I asked.

His face twisted into a 'hmmm'. 'Not from here, I can't. There'll be controls somewhere, though.'

I was worried. 'Without the force field, the gas will keep spreading and spreading. It'll knock everyone out! We need to find those controls.'

'Or –' the Doctor span lazily on his heels and pointed in a random direction – 'we shut off the gas. And I wouldn't be at all surprised if force field controls and sleepy gas source are both at the same place.'

'Probably the dome we entered through.'

'Probably, yes.' He took in a deep breath.

'What are you doing?' I yelped, as he staggered slightly.

'Just… checking… direction… of gas,' he said, slightly sheepishly, still reeling on the spot. But after a few seconds he recovered and called, 'This way!'

We decided to leave the unconscious bodies where they were. Not only would it be difficult for us to carry them, we were actually heading towards the source of the gas (or so we hoped), so it was safer for them there.

I don't know how long it took to walk back to the dome. I was half back in that dreamlike world again. There were moments when I would have given in to sleep if the Doctor hadn't been there to tell me to keep going. As it was, I think Elvis practically carried me the last half mile. Well, sometimes it's OK being a damsel in distress. At least it saves your legs.

I re-entered the world of consciousness to see a bald man looking down on me. My muddled thought processes went 'Sontaran? Silence? Jean-Luc?' until my head cleared and I realised it was Elvis. 'Well, we needed to bung up that nozzle,' said the Doctor, indicating Elvis's trademark quiff, now inserted into a hole halfway up the wall. 'Luckily Madame Tussauds don't use superglue to stick their wigs on.'

'The gas'll still seep out though,' I said. 'We have to find where it's coming from and shut it off.'

And so the three of us strode forward into the glass building: a purposeful approach that might have looked more impressive had our trio not consisted of an ancient Time Lord in a bow tie, a swishy-frocked heroine and a bald, plastic, alien Elvis Presley.

The Doctor had taken note of the nozzle's location and was now weaving his way through the honeycomb building to find its source. We went through room after room, tracking it nearer and nearer. 'Just through here!' said the Doctor eventually – and stopped.

The wall ahead wasn't made of glass, it was built of something black and yellow. No – it *was* made of glass. I realised that the black and yellow was moving. Crawling. Flying. On the other side of the wall was a solid mass of insects. Somewhere in the middle of them were the controls we needed to reach.

'The room's full of wasps!' I exclaimed.

The Doctor shook his head. 'They're too big for wasps. Giant hornets, if I'm not mistaken. The most venomous stingers of all. Well, you can't say that's not a good defence. Go in there and you'd be smothered in minutes. Not sure if even my system could cope with a few hundred stings.' He screwed up his nose. 'At the very least, it would *really* hurt.'

'They wouldn't affect Elvis, though,' I said, at the exact same moment that Elvis said, 'They wouldn't hurt me none.'

We looked at each other. 'That's settled, then.'

The Doctor sprang to action. 'Right! River, you get out of here.'

'Er, no,' I said.

'Er, *yes*,' he said. I do like it when he's masterful. That's master without a capital M, by the way. 'When

Elvis opens the door, a few hornets are going to get out,' he elaborated. 'Hopefully they're happy, happy hornets who don't want to sting anyone, but just in case they've got out of bed on the wrong side, I'd rather you were out of their way.'

'And you?'

'I'll be all right, as long as not too many get out. I have to stay close to give Elvis instructions on how to disable the systems.'

Well, I didn't much like the idea, but I complied. I only went as far as the next room, though. Thanks to the glass walls I at least had some idea of what was going on, distorted as the views were. I found the Doctor's confiscated picnic basket under a desk and fished out one of the remaining sandwiches to pass the time.

The Doctor's voice drifted through to me every now and then. 'Turn that dial up to ten! Now hit that switch! Cut the green wire!'

And then, just as I'd finished my sandwich and moved on to a cream horn, another voice joined his. 'What are you doing?!'

There was a note of hysteria in the voice. Through the warped glass Melissa – the new arrival was Melissa, of course – looked a hundred feet tall, the Doctor tiny beside her. There was something in her hand; it may have been a gun.

I hunkered down near the door, trying to make myself as inconspicuous as possible should she look my way. Always preserve the element of surprise in case it's needed.

She had spotted Elvis. 'How can he survive in there?'

'Oh, plastic man, nothing to worry about,' I heard the Doctor say. 'He's just dismantling your sleeping gas system. Some form of ultra-poppy extract, I expect? Might as well use the plants for everything, after you've got them so well fertilised.'

'You must stop him.'

'Sorry, no. You're the one who needs to stop.' The Doctor raised his voice. 'Elvis, keep on doing what you're doing, please.'

Now she raised her hand. Yes, definitely a gun. 'Stop him or I'll shoot.'

'No deal,' said the Doctor. 'You see, you're probably going to shoot me anyway. Can't let me go and tell the authorities what's going on here, what you make your extra-special fertiliser out of. But if we manage to sabotage your machine, there's at least a chance that the others out there will get away. Keep going, Elvis!'

'I will shoot!' she shrieked, and I believed her. I opened the door and flung the first thing to hand at her. The picnic basket.

You know how people use 'throw like a girl' as an insult? It wouldn't be an insult if the girl they were talking about was me. Because I throw like a demon. Yes, the basket distracted Melissa. But I threw it so hard and so fast that it smashed into the glass wall beside her.

Jam sandwiches and sticky buns and fizzy pop rained down on Melissa's head as the wall shattered and a thousand thousand hungry – and angry – hornets flew at her.

The Doctor dashed through the door towards me and I slammed it behind him. I couldn't see Melissa through the glass, only curtains of insects. The Doctor instinctively turned back, ready to dive back into the fray, but I took his arm. 'Elvis will get her out,' I said.

And eventually there he was, those magic hips swaggering towards us, a small body held in his waxen arms. I opened the door to let him through, shutting it swiftly before too many hornets joined them. A few buzzed disorientedly around, but paid no attention to us.

The Doctor looked at her. 'I'm sorry. That much venom in so short a time – she didn't have a chance.' He sighed. 'Come on. Let's get out of here.'

When it comes to adventures, the Doctor's very much a *wham-bam-thank-you* man. No hanging around afterwards.

'Shouldn't we...' began Elvis, who hadn't been around at the end of one of the Doctor's little jaunts before.

I shook my head. 'You've stopped the sleep gas, we'll take down the force field that's around this place, everyone wakes up and leave. We'll go home for tea and—' I broke off. I'd just remembered why we'd come here in the first place. Elvis's last hurrah.

'I'm staying,' he said.

'I know you wanted to spend your last days here...' I began, but Elvis stopped me.

'Nuh-huh. That's not why I'm staying. This stuff –' he gestured around him, which meant he was pretty much pointing at a few hornets and a dead woman covered in jam, but I took his meaning – 'is important for humanity. I'm going to keep it going.'

'But the Nestenes…'

The Doctor burst out laughing and clapped Elvis on the back. 'Yes! Brilliant! Well done that Auton. Of course, if we put the force field back up around this place, he'll be perfectly safe.'

'Er, on the subject of fertiliser…' I began.

'I think I'll find a new source,' he said.

I avoided the next Nestene invasion – well, all that 'is it a hand? No, it's a gun!' gets tedious after a while – but I did take a quick peek to see that Elvis had got through intact. I needn't have worried. 'Fans go "Wild in the Country" for Plastic Elvis!' was one of the headlines I spotted, and it turned out that his 'Benefit for Bees' concerts were great hits. I popped along to one – incognito – and cheered at his 'I Got Stung' (sung as bees swarmed around him) and 'It's Now Or Never' (waking up the world to what's going on re: insects). He was making quite an impact, and I'd never seen his plastic face look so happy. When he finished off with 'Peace In The Valley' and 'This Is My Heaven', I knew things were OK.

I was leaving the gig (with my jar of 'Money Honey' from the gift shop – all proceeds to help the bees) when I heard someone clearing their throat behind me. I turned, and so did everyone else, as Elvis the Auton began singing 'Are You Lonesome Tonight?', his eyes fixed on mine.

I listened, and realised that he'd put his plastic finger on something unalterable in my life. Whatever happened, whoever I was with, there would always be a sense in which I was lonesome. But it was something I would – and could – live with.

When he'd finished, I walked over and placed a hand on his smooth, hard cheek. 'I'm all shook up,' I told him. 'That's the wonder of you.' Then I kissed him. 'For ol' time's sake,' I said. Then I walked away.

River Song has left the building.

A Gamble with Time
Steve Lyons

It was the summer of 2016, in a city called London.

That's on Earth, in case I haven't mentioned it before.

On this summer morning, London was in the grip of an electrical storm.

What struck me, as I pushed my way along the West End's crowded pavements, was how little people cared. Most kept their heads down, just getting on with the daily grind of living. Occasionally, someone would glance up at the blood-red sky, shot through with forks of lightning. They would shake their heads and tut-tut and wonder if it was actually going to rain.

I don't know what else I expected.

At this point in Earth's history, if I'd told the cynical Londoners and the oblivious tourists around me that the storm was caused by alien intervention, that the universe of time and space was tearing itself apart, they would probably have rolled their eyes and sighed, 'Not again!'

Only one person, other than me, knew the truth.

His name was Martin Flint. He was a 46-year-old insurance salesman, living alone in a suburban basement flat that he could barely afford.

At ten o'clock that morning, he was waiting on the doorstep of his local bookmakers when it opened. He was wearing dark brown leather-uppers, no socks and a crumpled suit jacket over a pair of striped hospital pyjamas.

The bookie barely spared him a glance. He had seen worse.

What did surprise him was when Martin produced a debit card and insisted on placing every penny in his bank account – which came to a little under £1500 – on a single horse, an outside bet, to win.

You're wondering, Dear Diary, how I know this.

It began, as things so often do, with the Doctor.

He arrived at my door to pick me up. I have told him to stop doing that. I'm perfectly capable of managing my own escapes.

He was in his bow-tie-and-chin incarnation. As I would later learn, he hadn't been to Lake Silencio yet. If he had, he'd have known why showing his face – any of his faces – in Stormcage was a terrible idea.

To be fair to him, he had come in disguise.

Being less fair, the disguise was a twentieth-century British bobby's helmet. He seemed to think this rendered him unrecognisable. A square of psychic paper and a gormless expression can work miracles – luckily for him.

Behind the guards' backs, he doffed the headgear and pointed to his grinning face as if revealing his identity to me.

The guards agreed, with some misgivings, to hand me over to him – as long as we were shackled together. I certainly had no problem with that. The Doctor did his best to avoid my gaze as he applied the handcuffs. Dear Diary, how I love it when I can turn him bright red with a look.

We approached the exit at a measured pace, aware of eyes and camera lenses upon us. As we left the guards' earshot, I whispered sidelong to my escort: 'Nice bracelets. They look familiar.'

'You said we'd find a use for them,' he whispered back to me.

'Don't I just get you the best birthday presents?'

'River,' said the Doctor, gravely. 'I need your help.'

'You always did.'

'I've lost someone. A human person. I need you to find him. "Lost" is the wrong word, actually. I've *misplaced* him. I know where he is, but I can't get to him. There was this giant, green alien slug, you see, and—'

He was interrupted by a wailing alarm.

By now, we've both learned to run first and ask questions later.

This gave us a head start before the shooting began. Not that it helped us much. With gunfire closing around us from every direction, we ducked into an empty bathroom. The Doctor sonically melted the lock, which bought us a minute or two.

There was no other way out, of course – except for one. The Doctor brandished his screwdriver again and removed our handcuffs. He wrapped a device about my wrist to replace them. I recognised it as a vortex manipulator. Well, I would. I have one just like it myself.

'Martin Flint,' he said, loudly, over the sound of guards hammering at the door.

'Who?'

'On July the seventh 2016, 2.38 p.m., he stumbled into a vortex rift. In a car park off Great Russell Street.'

'That was careless.'

'He'd have been thrown back in time. Not very far. Somewhere between eight and ten hours. I need you to find him, keep an eye on him until time catches up with him. Make sure he doesn't do anything stupid – like contacting his younger self or telling everyone what happens in *Deal or No Deal* or—'

'You want me to babysit for you!' I arched an eyebrow.

The Doctor nodded happily. 'That is essentially it, yes. Don't worry, Martin's had a tiring day, so he'll probably sleep through.'

It had grown ominously quiet outside.

The guards, I imagined, had called for a sonic blaster, which would put a square hole through the door in seconds. It's on my Christmas list. The Doctor aimed his screwdriver at the vortex manipulator, and I realised he was about to operate it remotely. 'Did we miss the part where I agreed to this?' I protested.

'I thought we'd skip that part, save time.'

'What about you?' I asked him. 'Those guards will shoot you on sight. How will you get out of here?'

He grinned at me. He adjusted his policeman's helmet to a jauntier angle. 'River Song,' he said, 'I thought you'd recognised me.'

He thumbed a stud on his screwdriver.

Its emitter lit up green, the device on my wrist hummed to life – and I felt a terrible wrenching sensation as the bathroom, the Stormcage Containment Facility and the whole of the fifty-second century AD faded around me.

Next thing I knew, I was stumbling across a cobbled surface.

Vortex travel usually isn't so rough – except on my hair, but don't get me started on that. Something was wrong. Looking up at the sky, I confirmed it.

'Oh, Doctor,' I groaned, 'you arrange the most romantic getaways.'

I was in a tiny car park, between the backs of office buildings. It had two spaces – for the use, according to a gleaming sign, of employees of Dead Cert Investments – and a cluster of bins of various colours. Both spaces were currently empty.

I was in the right place, it seemed, but at the wrong time.

It wasn't 4.38 in the morning. It was too light for that, even with the storm raging overhead. I could hear the grumbling of rush-hour traffic from nearby streets.

The storm must have thrown me off course. I didn't dare try again.

Had I even arrived on the right day?

I was being watched.

A man had emerged from a fire exit door in one corner. He was standing at the top of a short flight of steps, behind a rail. He was middle-aged, short, balding, overweight, wearing an old-fashioned business suit with a waistcoat and fob watch.

'I'm sorry,' I said. 'I'm looking for a… friend. I don't suppose you know him. Martin Flint? He was here this morning.'

The man continued to glare at me, disdainfully, through a pair of round-rimmed glasses. I wondered how long he had been there.

Dear Diary, you're ahead of me at this point. You know this man is more than he appears to be, else why draw attention to him? I lacked the benefit of dramatic foreshadowing, however. I apologised again and left.

I made for the main road. I searched the pockets of my grey prison coveralls as I walked. I had you, Dear Diary, a pen and a tube of hallucinogenic lipstick, which I was saving for a special occasion. Had I known I was going on an adventure today, I would have been better prepared.

I'd have dressed more stylishly, at least.

I had to find Martin Flint as soon as possible. I had to find out what he had done to cause the time storm, and I had to fix it – if I could.

I wished the Doctor had told me more about him – if not an address, then an age, an occupation, his height, the colour of his eyes, anything. It was difficult to question passers-by about him without a description.

Not much point searching phone books or the worldwide web either, I concluded. If only his parents had been more imaginative when they named him…

I got my first break talking to a newsstand owner.

He had opened up at seven. An ambulance had sped past him as he had arrived fifteen minutes early. He was sure it had pulled out of the side street leading to the car park. I had him tell me the names of the nearest hospitals.

With a little wheedling – and crocodile tears for a 'missing fiancé' – I persuaded him to let me use his telephone.

Thirty-seven minutes later, I dumped a stolen moped in an ambulance bay. I mentally thanked the courier who had left it at the kerbside, unattended, complete with keys and helmet. I'm sure, if I'd had time to explain why I needed it, he would have minded less. At least he might have moderated his language.

I had already established that Martin Flint had been brought here. I asked for more details at the admissions desk. I was asked in turn if I was a relative of his. Being familiar with this time and place, I had expected this and had rehearsed an expedient lie. 'Yes, I am,' I said.

It was outside visiting hours, but no one tried to stop me as I strode onto Martin Flint's ward as if I'd every right to be there. I found an empty bed with his name on a whiteboard behind it. A newspaper was spread across the sheets. I picked it up and checked the date on it: *Thursday 7 July 2016.*

With a twinge of anxiety, I flagged down a passing nurse. I pointed out to her that one of her patients was missing.

She wasn't overly concerned, at first. 'He can't have gone far,' she insisted, cheerfully. She indicated a half-open cupboard by the bedside. A pair of crumpled grey trousers and a white shirt lay folded on its shelf. A battered brown leather briefcase occupied the space underneath them.

I crouched to take a closer look.

'He was feeling much brighter, anyhow. He'd had some sort of blackout, but we couldn't find anything physically wrong with him. We're sending him for a scan this afternoon, but he can probably go home after that. You *are* a relative?'

'Shoes,' I said, checking under the bed. 'Where are his shoes?'

Well, there followed something of a kerfuffle.

Bathrooms were searched and questions asked. The patient in the adjacent bed to Martin's testified that something in the newspaper had agitated him. 'He kept asking me what day it was, like he couldn't remember, poor blighter.'

Someone else had actually seen him slipping away, with a suit jacket bundled under his arm. His hands had been shaking. 'I just thought he was stepping outside for a ciggie.' A porter was despatched to check, but came back empty-handed.

I took advantage of the empty nurses' station, in the meantime, to sneak a look at the computer records. Someone had been logged in when they were rudely distracted. It only took a few keystrokes to bring up Martin Flint's address.

I hoped my borrowed moped hadn't been clamped or towed yet.

Martin lived midway along – and underneath – a row of Victorian terraces, with white stucco work and bay windows.

I pulled up across the street at 10.44 a.m. My timing could hardly have been better. Someone was just leaving the flat, fumbling with a deadlock key. *The man himself?* Could I have been that lucky?

This man was in his mid-to-late forties, matching the age I had gleaned from Martin's hospital records. His shoulders were slumped as if bearing the weight of the world. He wore a crumpled grey suit with brown shoes – but it was the briefcase that really gave him away.

He carried a battered brown leather briefcase, like the one I had seen at the hospital. *No*, I thought, *not like the one at the hospital*…

I had found Martin Flint, all right – but it was the wrong Martin Flint. This was the younger model – younger by between eight and ten hours – the one that belonged in this moment. He was walking at a hurried pace with his head down, northward along the street, towards the tube station around the corner.

I was torn between searching his flat for clues to his future-self's whereabouts or trailing him. The former option, I realised, could leave me with nothing.

I decided to hang on to my only lead.

I hopped off my bike and fell into step behind Flint-the-younger. We hadn't gone very far at all when another figure rounded the corner ahead of us.

I corrected myself again: *the same figure.*

This Martin Flint was wearing dark brown leather-uppers, no socks and a crumpled suit jacket over a pair of striped hospital pyjamas.

The younger Martin, paying little attention to his surroundings, hadn't noticed his older self yet. Flint-the-elder, however, stumbled to a halt directly in his path. He was staring at his less dishevelled twin, wild-eyed.

I increased my pace – not by enough, I hoped, for the younger Martin to notice me as I overtook him. I got between the two of them, flinging out my arms to block their view of each other. 'Darling!' I cried. I swept up to the older Martin, threw a crushing hug around him and planted my lips on his.

The younger Martin glanced up as he passed us, but didn't recognise the back of his own head. I held the lip lock until he had turned the corner, at which point its recipient pulled away from me.

'What are you doing?' he spluttered. 'Who are you?' For the record, Dear Diary, when I snog a complete stranger, I usually get a much better reaction.

I fixed Martin Flint with a confident gaze, a gaze that said I knew more than I really did. 'The Doctor sent me—'

'Um, who? I don't think I know any—'

'—and I can tell from the startled-rabbit look in your eyes that you know who I mean, so don't even try to lie to me.' I indicated the corner around which Martin Flint-the-younger had vanished. 'Where is he going?'

'I… He… I had to call into the office for a couple of hours. Then I had a… an interview in town this afternoon, only I…' His shoulders sagged. He rubbed his puffy, red eyes with his thumbs. He was unwashed and unshaven.

'I was in a… Was I in a car park? I saw a… a…'

'A giant, green alien slug?' I prompted, helpfully.

'And a man, there was a man there, with a—'

'Chin. So, your flat should be empty for the rest of the day?'

Martin blinked at me. 'How do you know I live alone?'

'Sweetie, where do you want me to start?' I said.

'I'm not… I'm not going mad, am I?' Martin Flint asked me.

'You'd be a better judge of that than I would.'

'But… this is Thursday, yes? Thursday…'

'July the seventh.'

He sank onto a battered-looking couch, with creaking springs and old stains in the fabric. 'But I… I've already—'

'—lived through Thursday July the seventh once. I know. I just saw you doing it, remember? Welcome back.'

I wandered into a cluttered kitchenette. I rooted out a pair of clean glasses from the crockery piles on the draining board and filled them from the tap.

I could see Martin through the serving hatch, though he had his back to me. He was hunched up, still trying to grasp the ungraspable.

'So, you… How do you know about—?'

'—your future? Oh, Martin, you know how it is these days. Spoilers everywhere you look, you can't avoid them. I blame the internet – for that and for making cats believe they rule the world.'

I pushed a glass of cold water into his hands. He took it from me, but didn't look at it. 'Did you… come back in time too? Did you follow me here?'

'Well, someone had to,' I averred. 'Do you know what would have happened if I hadn't just kept you from meeting yourself?'

'No, what would have happened?'

'That… depends. Anything from an incurable case of déjà vu to the destruction of the time continuum. Right now, I'm leaning firmly towards the latter – or haven't you seen the sky out there?'

'The storm?' Martin grimaced as if the effort of remembering hurt him. 'You're saying I…? No, that can't be, because your Doctor friend, I remember him saying that the storm was caused by the… the monster.'

I sat beside him. 'The storm happened yesterday too? I mean, today? You remember the storm from today, from the first time you lived through it?'

'Yes, yes, that's what I'm saying. It may have… I'm not sure, it may be a little worse this time than… Is that possible? How is that possible?'

I took a sip of water. I swilled it around my mouth as I thought.

So, the Doctor had been involved in Martin's 'accident'.

That much had almost gone without saying, hadn't it? Why else couldn't he have come back here himself? He can be a real stickler about his Laws of Time – when it suits him. Having two Martin Flints in London on the same day was bad enough. Having two Doctors on top of that…

Excuse me, Dear Diary, while I conjure with that image for a moment.

I asked Martin to tell me everything, from the beginning. 'On second thoughts,' I said, 'forget the beginning. Go from this morning.'

'Do you mean "this morning" the first time or…?'

'After you fell into the rift. You woke up and…?'

'The car park. I was still in the car park, only it… The sun was rising. I thought I must have lain there all night. It was cold, so cold and I couldn't remember… just flashes of… I must have blacked out again. The next thing I recall, I was warm, in a hospital bed. The nurses said I was lucky someone found me when they

did. There was a radio playing on the ward, and that…
that's how I knew…'

'That it was Thursday morning all over again.'

'I thought I was going mad.'

'I can imagine.'

'And the papers too… I was so confused. I had to get
out of there. I had to get back to… to the real world, to
somewhere I knew. I discharged myself.'

'Escaped, you mean.'

'I grabbed my jacket and shoes and slipped away
while no one was looking. I found my way to the tube. I
came home. I don't know what I expected to find here.'

'Oh, trust me, you got lucky – if I say so myself.'

'I just want to… I don't know, go to sleep and wake
up tomorrow, Friday morning, when there isn't another
"me" out there and everything makes sense again.'

'And that's all?'

'What do you mean?'

I regarded him through narrowed eyes. 'You've
nothing else to tell me?'

'Nothing,' insisted Martin, but he wouldn't meet my
gaze.

'So, you came straight here from the hospital. You
didn't take any diversions?'

'I already said.'

I looked at the carriage clock on Martin's
mantelpiece. It told me that the time was 11.03. I had
left the hospital after he did, but beaten him home. We
had taken different modes of transport, though. He
could have been telling me the truth.

My every instinct told me otherwise.

'Martin, listen to me, this is important. You aren't supposed to be here, you know that. Every action you take in the past has consequences, and they can—'

'What about you?' he interrupted me, with a flash of belligerence. 'You shouldn't be here either, should you?'

'No,' I confessed, 'I shouldn't, but I know what I'm doing. I know which butterflies not to tread on – and, Martin, I'm not the one crossing my own time stream. You've heard of the grandfather paradox?'

'I'm not sure. Is that the one where—?'

'You must have seen *Back to the Future*.'

His eyes widened. 'That… Is that what you're worried about? But you saw everything that happened. I didn't talk to him. The other me, he didn't see me. I mean, *I* didn't even see me. He didn't… I won't…'

His brow furrowed in the familiar manner of a time-traveller juggling tenses and personal pronouns. I had to admit, though, he had a point. He *hadn't* interacted with himself. I had headed him off before he could. So, whatever Martin Flint was keeping from me – and I knew there was something – how important could it be?

I stood and crossed the room, to a back window. It looked out onto an austere yard with a few flowers withering in planter boxes. The building must have been on a slope, as the yard – and the alleyway behind it – were level with Martin's living room. Steps swept down into the former from the flat above.

If I craned my neck, I could see a patch of roiling red sky. *Was* the storm getting worse, I wondered?

The best thing might have been to let Martin sleep, as he wanted. Watch over him for just over three and a half hours, then slip away. Trust that, whatever else was happening out there, the Doctor would handle – indeed, had already handled – it. A simple babysitting job, then, as advertised.

I turned back to Martin. He was hugging his knees, staring blankly into the mid-distance. 'Tell me about the Doctor and the giant, green alien slug,' I said. 'Tell me what happened in the car park.'

A shadow passed the front window, at that moment, as someone descended the steps to Martin's door. A sudden harsh buzzing noise startled Martin, who leapt out of his seat.

'Don't answer it,' I cautioned him. 'Martin Flint isn't home, remember? He's sitting on a train on his way into the office, then he has—'

My words fell on deaf ears, needless to say.

'It's Mr Smith!' cried Martin, peering out through a grubby net curtain.

'Who?'

'It's Mr… What is he doing here? This could be important. I have to…'

He bustled out into the tiny hallway before I could stop him. He opened the door. I heard his voice and another – a soft, rasping voice – exchanging pleasantries. Then Martin returned, with his visitor in tow. 'Mr Smith, this is, uh…'

'River,' I said. 'River Song.'

Neither of us made a move to shake hands. We sized each other up with recognition – and suspicion – in our eyes as Martin burbled on, oblivious.

'And this is, ah, Mr Smith. I had… I have an interview with him this afternoon, remember I mentioned? A second interview. He runs a business in town called—'

'—Dead Cert Investments,' I deduced.

Dear Diary, it was of course the man with the glasses, from the car park.

Martin glanced down at his hospital pyjamas, self-consciously. 'Ah, yes. I should probably go and… Make yourself at home, Mr Smith, I'll only be a…' He hurried away across the hall into – I assumed – his bedroom.

In the meantime, 'Mr Smith' and I circled each other warily.

'So, you found your "friend", Ms Song. I'm glad for you.'

'Yes, thank you, I did.'

His lips twisted into a smile, which stopped short of his steely grey eyes. 'I thought I ought to call on Mr Flint, see that everything was… as it should be.'

'How thoughtful of you. Tell me, Mr Smith,' I said coolly, 'what exactly does Dead Cert Investments do? No, let me guess – you deal in futures.'

'That would be an area of interest to you, I take it?'

'You could say I've dabbled.'

'Perhaps you should call in for an interview yourself. That is, if your current employers would have no objections?'

'Oh, I don't work for— Ah.' Mr Smith was staring pointedly at my right wrist. My sleeve had ridden up over the vortex manipulator.

His expression left me in no doubt that he recognised it for what it was.

His hand went to his hip. I was already diving for cover behind the couch.

Suddenly, he had a gun, as if snatched from an invisible holster. It was a stubby white blaster that certainly hadn't been produced on this world in this year. He fired a beam of energy, which seared over my head and melted a wall mirror into slag.

He barged around the side of the couch and fired again.

He burned a circular hole in Martin's carpet.

I had already scrambled out of his way. I snatched an ashtray from the coffee table and hurled it like a discus. It struck my attacker on the temple, throwing off his next shot, which destroyed the front window. I threw myself after the ashtray. I tackled Mr Smith to the ground while he was dazed.

He was stronger than he looked. He managed to throw me off him. He scrabbled to retrieve his dropped gun. I caught hold of his belt, or so I thought. I tried to drag him back towards me, but something came away in my hand instead. At the same time, there was a flash of green light and Mr Smith's appearance… changed.

I was holding a small, spherical device with a control pad and a tiny lens set into it: a hologram projector.

I was looking at a fat, green monster, its soft tissue shimmering with moisture. I didn't know the species, but the description was certainly familiar.

It reared up on its tail, with a sucking sound, looming over me. A pair of twitching feelers sprouted from its head, with blazing red eyes at their tips. The monster wore a mechanical mantle, from which a pair of cybernetic arms extended. One of these held its blaster, from which a snaking silver tube also plugged into the mantle.

I dived into the kitchenette, as the giant slug strafed the room behind me.

I looked for a weapon: a knife, anything I could use. Trust the Doctor to send me into danger unarmed! I swear, I love that man but sometimes I want to slap him. I heard a startled voice from the outer room, then a scuffle and a strangulated squeak. Martin was back – and, of course, the giant slug had him.

I glimpsed him through the serving hatch, dressed in a suit and shirt that looked exactly the same as the old ones. At least he was wearing socks now.

'Come out of there, Time Agent,' the monster hissed. Its voice, which sounded like Mr Smith's voice, emerged from a grille in its mantle as the eyes on its feelers blinked furiously. It held Martin Flint with a mechanical arm around his throat and was pressing the gun to his head. 'Or watch as I kill your friend.'

'It was you,' Martin whimpered. 'Mr Smith, you were the monster all—'

'Oh, I'm no Time Agent,' I said hurriedly, talking over him, 'but I am the one that should be making threats. I have…' I had nothing. What I needed was inspiration. I cast around for it. *A giant slug,* I thought, *and I'm in a kitchen. Why not?* 'I have a big bag of salt and I'm not afraid to use it.'

A shudder convulsed the slug's body from feelers to tail.

I seized the initiative. 'Look,' I said, 'Mr… actually, what do I call you now? You don't look very much like a "Smith" to me.'

'Gharjhax,' the creature slurped. 'I am Gharjhax, prince-in-exile of the Mighty Garden Empire of the Gastropodic Alliance, and I—'

'I'm sure – and I'm a madwoman with a vortex manipulator, who turned up in your car park when I did entirely by accident. So, you've been doing a bit of time-travelling yourself? I'm hardly in a position to criticise, and I didn't come here to stop you.' *So far, so true.*

'And I… I didn't mean to…' Martin pitched in. 'I came for my interview, saw you fighting with that Doctor fellow in the car park and I—'

I interrupted him again. 'How about this?' I suggested. 'You let Martin go, I give you back your hologram projector. You'd find it tricky, running your business without it. Your clients would stare. We make the swap and the three of us walk out of here, without anyone shooting anyone else. We go our separate ways and never—'

'Agreed,' said Gharjhax – too quickly, I thought.

We made the exchange, all the same.

I tossed the projector to Gharjhax, deliberately high. He pushed his hostage away from him as he reached to catch the device. Martin stumbled into the kitchenette, trembling. I was already at the back door, fumbling with the lock. I bundled Martin out into the yard before he could say a word and told him to run.

Gharjhax appeared behind me with his blaster raised. I knew I couldn't trust him. 'On reflection—' he began. I'm sure it would have been a suitably pithy remark. I didn't wait to hear it either. I hadn't found a bag of salt, but I had seen a half-full cellar on one of the worktops. I shook it in the slug's direction.

He squealed – more, I think, in fear than in pain, as only a few grains could have hit him – and his shot went wild. It struck a strip light on the ceiling, precipitating a fierce electrical shower between us.

I raced after Martin, through the yard. He was waiting for me behind the gate and I cannoned into him. 'Keep running, you idiot!' I screamed at him – and we ran.

Martin wanted to go back to his flat.

He fretted about the open back door and the melted window. He said there had been burglaries in the area. I told him that, if Gharjhax set eyes on him again, he'd lose more than his possessions.

'You're the one he wants to kill,' he responded, sullenly.

Dear Diary, he wasn't wrong.

So much for not treading on butterflies. I knew now that Gharjhax had either seen or detected my arrival in 2016 – whereupon I had given him Martin Flint's name and thus told him exactly where he could find me later.

Well, how was I to know he would have Martin's address on file?

The blood-red hue of the sky had definitely deepened, while lightning struck more frequently and more violently than ever. Thunder rumbled ominously in the distance. 'Gharjhax has an appointment with the Doctor this afternoon,' I said, half to myself. 'If he misses that because of me…'

Another thought, an even worse one, hit me.

I grabbed Martin's hand and started running again, ignoring his howl of protest. I dragged him towards the tube station. 'We're going to your office.'

'But my… my other self is there, and you said—'

'I know what I said, Martin. This is about what *you* said.'

'What do you mean? I don't…'

'You as good as read Gharjhax his fortune back there. You warned him that something bad is about to happen to him – and that you, your younger self, will be involved. What would you do, armed with that information, if you were a giant, green, time-travelling, homicidal alien slug?'

'I… I'd…' Martin turned pale.

We reached the train station. I persuaded my befuddled companion to buy me a travelcard, and we waited on an open-air platform.

'I should call him,' said Martin, suddenly. 'Me. I should warn me about...' He winced as he patted himself down. 'My phone. I left it in my briefcase in the hospital. Is there a payphone? Can you see a payphone anywhere?'

'Phoning yourself is never a good idea,' I advised him. 'Just imagine for a second how that conversation would go – and anyway, our train is here.'

It was just pulling in, in a screeching huff. At this time of day, this far from the city centre, its carriages were almost empty. I asked Martin how long the journey would take us. 'On a good day, three-quarters of an hour,' was his answer.

Could Gharjhax get there any faster, I wondered? First, he had to put two and two together, then find Martin's work address – unless he had it with him – and the car park behind his office had been empty of vehicles, I recalled.

It occurred to me that he could have been on the train alongside us, in a new holographic disguise.

The next forty-five minutes passed achingly slowly.

Martin worked on the fourth floor of a concrete and glass building, not far from the Barbican Centre. Approaching at a run, we saw a police car and an ambulance parked outside. *That could mean anything*, I told myself.

My heart sank at the sight of a familiar moped overturned outside the doors.

I chose not to wait for the lift.

By the time we had surmounted the stairs, Martin was panting and sweating. I saw this as a good thing, as it meant he couldn't say much. His office was a hive of activity – there were paramedics and a couple of constables present – so the last thing I needed was him blurting out something he shouldn't.

Gharjhax had left his mark here. There were scorch marks on the walls and an ionised smell in the air. Computer monitors and keyboards had been melted into new and interesting shapes. Chairs had been overturned.

Shell-shocked office workers sat in huddles. Some of them were receiving medical attention, but none appeared seriously hurt. Either Gharjhax was a truly terrible shot – and I can't dismiss that possibility – or he hadn't been shooting to kill.

One worker was notably missing.

'I'm looking for Martin Flint,' I announced. 'Where is he?'

A pale-faced teenager in an ill-fitting suit blinked at me. 'That's him, right there. He's standing behind you.'

'Right. Yes. Obviously. What I meant was—'

'Martin!'

The shout came from two directions at once, and echoed around us as a whisper: 'Martin... Martin... Martin...' Suddenly, we were the centre of attention – and people were converging upon us, brimming with questions. Was Martin OK? Where had he been? What did he know about the monster that had crashed into their lives?

'It was looking for you,' someone clarified for us, helpfully. 'It asked for you by name. By name! What the hell is going on, Martin?'

I improvised. 'He can't talk. He's had a shock. What did the monster do to him?' I hadn't seen a body, thankfully. 'Take him hostage? Did it look at any point as if he might have been – oh, let's say – disintegrated at all?'

Martin let out a strangulated whine.

'He wasn't here,' the pale-faced teenager offered. 'That's why the monster shot up the place. It said, if we didn't tell it where he was—'

'Not here?' Martin had found his voice. 'But that's impossible. I…'

'What did you tell it?' I asked.

'We had no choice. Sorry, Martin, but it would have killed us all.'

'Kath told it about your phone call,' someone else pitched in, 'from the bank. She said you'd gone to sort things out – but she didn't know which bank you'd gone to, not exactly. None of us did. So—'

I rounded on Martin. 'Which bank?'

'There's a branch near my flat, but I never…'

I cast around for an un-melted wall clock. It was 12.34.

'It's time we made that call,' I decided. I recovered a desk phone from the floor, checked that it was still working and thrust it into Martin's hands, keeping hold of the receiver. I instructed him to dial.

I listened to the ringback tone, wondering what I would say to Martin Flint when he answered. As it turned out, I didn't have to worry about that.

I heard a tinny rendition of a pop song from the 1980s, muffled but growing in volume as its source approached me. A smartly dressed young woman with her hair in disarray was carrying a familiar briefcase.

'You left in such a hurry, you forgot to take this with you. I tried to catch you up, but…' She handed the case to Martin, who rummaged behind a battered leather flap, produced a warbling mobile phone and shot me a helpless look.

More policemen were arriving, asking questions, scribbling in notebooks. I whisked Martin away from there, before they could hem us in. We escaped through an unwatched side door. As we clattered down four flights of stairs together, I warned my companion, 'You have a *lot* of explaining to do.'

'I've really done it, haven't I?' said Martin, morosely. 'Changed my own past. *Back to the Future*. What happens now? Do I start… fading away?' He squinted at his own hands, turning them over in front of him, wiggling his fingers.

'That might be the least of our problems,' I murmured.

We were perched on a low wall outside Liverpool Street Station, with railings behind us. I had done the calculations. We couldn't reach the bank, find Martin Flint-the-younger and get him to his job interview on time.

If Martin didn't make the interview, he couldn't fall into the vortex rift and return to this morning.

Everything would revert to how it had been. Martin would show up for his interview and fall into the rift again, tying history into a knot.

'He'll make it,' Martin Flint-the-elder insisted. 'He will. I really wanted that job. It meant more money, a lot more, and my first interview went really well, I really thought I had a chance. So, whatever the problem at the bank is, I'm sure—'

'What is the problem at the bank? Martin?'

'I don't know. How could I know?'

'What did you do? The truth, this time. I know there's something.'

He shifted uncomfortably. 'Sometimes, I suppose, the bank calls me about… what they call "unusual activity" on my account.'

'Such as?'

'I might have… I did… I placed a bet. A small bet. Maybe not so small…'

He cast me a sidelong glance. He must have seen the reproach in my eyes, because he went on the defensive. 'Well, how was I to know…? I checked the racing results before I left the office. In the hospital, I remembered, the winner of the 12.30, odds of sixteen-to-one… and didn't I deserve something after…?'

'You put all your money on a horse,' I summed up.

'I did. Yes.'

'A bookmaker let you do that?'

Martin shrugged. 'It took some persuading, but Geoff knows me – and he's taken enough off me in the past. He'll have laid off most of it with the big chains, anyway, so it's not as if he'll lose… I mean, it's not like I'm really…'

'Taking something that doesn't belong to you?'

Get me, Dear Diary, up on my moral high horse! The truth is, I don't care if Martin Flint – or a hundred giant, green alien slugs for that matter – enrich themselves using time travel, as long as they're careful. As long as they don't try to take too much. *Every action you take in the past has consequences…*

'Companies like that,' Martin mumbled, studying his shoes, 'a few thousand pounds is nothing, nothing at all, to them. They won't miss it.'

Lightning flashed directly above us. The fiercest thunderclap yet drowned out the droning traffic. The pair of us looked up, apprehensively. 'No,' I agreed with Martin, 'you're probably right about that. They probably won't.'

'You, um, said something this morning, about… destruction?'

'The destruction of the time continuum. Yes.'

'That would be… bad, wouldn't it?' I didn't feel I needed to answer that question. 'Is there anything we could possibly, you know, do about it?'

I wrenched my eyes away from the blood-red sky. I pulled myself together. 'There's always something,' I maintained, 'especially where the Doctor is concerned.'

'The Doctor?'

'I wasn't completely honest with you either. I have trodden on a few butterflies myself, in my time. Some very big butterflies.' *Lake Silencio, for one,* I was thinking. 'But the Doctor found a way to set things right. He always does.'

Martin Flint said, 'Oh.'

I frowned at him. 'Now what's wrong?'

'It's just that, I think… I might have saved the Doctor's life. In the car park. The monster was about to… and I… So, if I was never there…'

I took a deep breath. I told myself not to panic. My ears were filled with the sound of thunder. We were running out of options.

We returned to the place where – if you'll pardon my own mangled tenses, Dear Diary – it had all been about to begin.

Dead Cert Investments occupied an office above an empty shop unit on Great Russell Street. It was just as unimpressive from the front as it had been from the rear.

We had had some time to kill. It was 1.52 p.m. We were early.

'Take me through this again,' I demanded.

Martin obliged. 'I got here… will get here at 2.20. I buzzed and buzzed, but no one answered me.' He indicated a door entry system with three buttons. 'I thought maybe I was too early. I waited until half-past, my appointment time, but no one came. I began to wonder if I'd got the time right or the day or…'

'So, you decided to…?' I nudged him.

'Look around the back of the building, see if there was another door there.'

'Which there is,' I recalled. With a brisk stride, I led Martin down a familiar side street towards a familiar tiny, cobbled car park.

'So, this is where you saw them: Gharjhax and the Doctor.'

Martin nodded. 'I heard them shouting to begin with and I saw strange, flickering lights. I came around the corner of the building there, and the – Doctor? – was at the top of those steps by the door, while the monster—'

'The door. Was it open or closed?' I asked.

Martin's brow furrowed. 'It was… open, I think. No, closed. The door was closed. The door was definitely closed.'

I climbed the steps to the fire exit door, where I had seen 'Mr Smith' that morning. I stooped to examine it. There was no way to open it from this side. I pushed on the door, experimentally. It didn't yield. A sonic screwdriver would unlock it in a second, of course – as long as the wielder had that second.

'And Gharjhax,' I asked. 'Where was he?'

'He was here,' said Martin, from behind me. 'He was right here at the bottom of the steps. Is that…? Does that help?'

'It might,' I considered.

I reached into my pocket and took out my hallucinogenic lipstick. Considering what it cost me, this was not how I had envisaged using it. Needs must, though.

I scrawled a brief message, just three words long, in foot-high letters across the fire exit door. I added three kisses at the bottom, in lieu of a signature. I straightened up to admire my handiwork.

'What do we do now?' asked Martin.

'We wait,' I said, 'and we watch.'

'Oh. Is that all?'

'If we are quite spectacularly lucky, it might be.'

We found a hiding place behind the bins, which gave us a perfect view of the prospective arena. We crouched in nervous silence and listened to the storm.

Martin began to fidget. I admonished him with a fierce whisper. He had cramp in his leg, he whimpered. He forgot about it quickly enough, as we heard a soft cough and an approaching shuffle that sounded nothing like footsteps.

A short, round, suited figure appeared at the car park entrance.

He surveyed the cobbled yard through round-rimmed glasses. He checked his fob watch and nodded to himself in satisfaction. Then he turned and stepped back out into the street, out of our line of sight.

'That... that was him,' whispered Martin, unnecessarily. 'Mr Smith.'

I eased back the flap of Martin's briefcase, to check the time on his phone. It was 2.16 p.m. 'He's early.'

'What does that mean? Is that bad?'

'It means he's here. It means one member of our cast is in place awaiting his cue. Just two more to come. It means we have a chance.'

History, as the Doctor always says, is remarkably resilient. I only hoped it would prove to be resilient enough.

Speaking of the Doctor, he was our next arrival.

He sauntered onto the scene with his hands behind his back, whistling. He kicked away imaginary pebbles as he walked, while his head turned in every direction except towards Dead Cert Investments' back door. He could have been performing 'casual innocence' in a pantomime.

He cocked his head as if hearing a suspicious sound. He raised a finger to his chin in a study of contemplation. I think he muttered something to himself.

Who did he imagine was watching him, anyway? Other than Martin Flint and me, I mean. Oh, and of course the alien slug.

'Aha!' the Doctor exclaimed. He spun around, throwing out an arm dramatically, pointing at the door like an arrow. He straightened his back. He reached inside his jacket for his sonic screwdriver, and now his expression was deadly serious.

The performance was over.

He climbed the steps towards the door. As he did so, Martin grabbed my arm, digging his fingernails into it. I followed his frightened gaze. 'Mr Smith' had returned. He crept across the tiny car park. He had drawn his blaster and was training it upon his oblivious target's back.

Martin tensed, preparing to break cover. I placed my hand firmly on his shoulder, shaking my head. I prayed I was doing the right thing.

'Mr Smith' was right behind the Doctor now. I thought of all the past times we would never have had if he died here today. He had reached the fire exit door, however. He couldn't miss my lipstick message to him: LOOK BEHIND YOU.

He whirled around.

Gharjhax's weapon disappeared inside his holographic field.

'You must be the proprietor,' said the Doctor, 'Mr…?'

'Smith,' replied the disguised alien.

The Doctor grinned in recognition. 'Ooh, I use that alias as well. We could be fake-related. Let's see now. Hologram projector mounted in a cyber-mantle? The giveaway is the slithering sound you still make when you move. I'm—'

'I know who you are – Doctor!'

The Doctor's eyes narrowed for a moment. Then he continued, brightly: 'So, now that we've been introduced—'

'You aren't the first Time Agent to try to stop me!' Gharjhax hissed.

'I'm not a Time Agent,' said the Doctor.

'That's what the last one said.'

'But I *am* going to stop you.'

'That isn't going to happen.' 'Mr Smith' smiled his twisted smile again, and suddenly his gun was back. 'I've seen the future.' He squeezed the trigger.

At the same time, the Doctor activated his sonic screwdriver – and Gharjhax's true shape was revealed in a sickly green flash.

His cybernetic mantle was damaged. It was hissing, spitting, sparking – and an electrical crackle shot along the flexible connecting tube to his blaster. The weapon exploded, taking Gharjhax's mechanical right hand with it.

He reeled in horror. 'What did you *do*?'

'Design flaw on the Mantle 5000,' said the Doctor, almost apologetically. 'Loosen the right screws and you can short-circuit the control board, which—'

He broke off as Gharjhax released a chilling howl and lolloped towards him. He left a glistening, sticky-looking trail across the cobbles behind him.

The steps to the fire exit door slowed him down. The Doctor clambered up onto the railing and was about to jump when, suddenly, a second giant slug appeared directly beneath him. Its mantle was crackling too. It was missing a hand.

'Mr Smith, whatever your name is, listen to me,' the Doctor cried, turning from one giant slug to the other. 'I didn't realise – I should have realised – but your vortex manipulator is wired up to your mantle. It's—'

The first slug barged him into the brick wall behind him, winding him. The Doctor struggled desperately against it, but was pinned by the monster's sheer bulk.

Then, suddenly, the monster vanished – to reappear, I deduced, a few feet away and a few seconds ago – and the Doctor was freed, gasping for breath.

The remaining Gharjhax was gasping too.

His mantle was wreathed in coruscating energy, which was evidently causing him some pain. It was also discharging bolts in every direction. Martin and I recoiled as one struck a bright blue bin in front of us, erasing it from existence – at least, from present existence – and, Dear Diary, that wasn't even the worst of it.

The energy was clawing holes in the very air. The rifts opened for a second, two seconds at a time, and through them I caught glimpses of the vortex itself and had to turn my face away from it. 'Where are you, Martin Flint?' I murmured.

I heard the Doctor pleading: 'You have to let me close enough to repair—'

'No, get away from me!'

'You don't understand what—'

'You did this to me! You!' roared Gharjhax.

'The storm. You must have noticed the storm. It was raging long before I came along. You did that. Hopping into the future and back to make a profit – you punctured the space-time vortex like a colander. I can fix this, if you—'

'*Die, Doctor, die!*'

'I heard that,' Martin Flint – the one beside me, the wrong one – breathed. I didn't grasp his meaning at first. 'I was here,' he said, more urgently, 'when they said all that – the first time. I was *here*.' And, Dear Diary, my heart froze.

We squinted past the bursts of vortex energy and the rips in the air, at the car park entrance – the empty car park entrance. 'I should be here,' insisted Martin. 'I should be standing right there. *Where am I?*'

The Doctor had vaulted the railings, dropping onto the cobbles.

He danced around his enemy. He was trying to get close to him, but was repeatedly rebuffed by sparks of energy or thrashing mechanical arms.

He saw an opening – so he thought – and made a dive for it. Gharjhax's remaining cyber-hand caught him by the throat. The Doctor fell to his knees, trying desperately to speak, only able to wheeze and splutter. The giant slug's red eyes bulged out of his feelers, as his metal fingers tightened… and tightened…

'It's going to kill him,' squealed Martin. 'You have to do something!'

It took all the self-control I had to shake my head. 'I wish I could, Martin,' I said, 'but I can't. It can't be me.'

The Doctor had sent me here. He hadn't dared cross his own time stream. If I interfered directly in his past, however – that was almost as bad. Like Martin, I'd be altering the events that brought me here in the first place.

If I had to, I would do it and hang the consequences!

I had had a better idea, though. Dear Diary, it wasn't a very *nice* idea…

I turned to face Martin. I placed my hands on his stooped shoulders. 'Martin Flint saved the Doctor's life,' I reminded him. 'That's the way it happened – and the way it has to happen, if history is ever to be repaired.'

'But he… he isn't here!' Martin protested.

I looked him firmly in the eyes. 'Yes, Martin, he is.'

It took a second for comprehension to dawn on him. A succession of emotions crossed Martin Flint's eyes in a second. Horror came first, then fear, then resignation and finally – sooner than I had expected, to give him due credit – resolution.

Martin shifted his gaze back to the desperate struggle.

He was watching and waiting for his moment, the right moment – the *same* moment. Everything had to be exactly as it had been before.

Did he truly understand what he was about to do? I still wonder.

A normal man would have choked to death by now.

The Doctor's face was red and his eyes had glazed over.

Martin Flint made his move. He broke cover and shoulder-charged Gharjhax, with his battered leather briefcase raised between them like a shield. He broke his deadly grip on the Doctor and sent him reeling.

Gharjhax collided with the back wall of his own building. He must have dislodged something in his mantle – because, with one final pop and a puff of smoke, it died. The giant slug crumpled to the ground, unconscious or dead.

Martin was reeling too. The last tear in the universe gaped open beside him, hungrily, and he couldn't help himself, he stumbled into it. In a heartbeat, he was gone, and the tear sealed itself behind him – as if neither of them had existed.

The Doctor was back on his feet already, screwdriver in hand.

'No,' he moaned to himself. 'No, no, no, no.' He dropped into a crouch beside the prostrate Gharjhax and scanned him. He took a deep breath and let it go.

'You can come out now,' he said, quietly.

I stepped out from behind the bins. 'Hello, Sweetie.'

'River Song. Why is it that, whenever there's an existential threat to the universe of time and space, you always seem to be involved?'

'Actually, I've just done you a huge favour. How is he?'

'He'll live. I'll give UNIT a bell. They can send a team to collect him within fifteen minutes. So, if I call ten minutes ago…'

The Doctor stood. He turned to face me. 'I'm more concerned about your friend – what was his name? He just stumbled into—'

'—a vortex rift. Yes. He'll have been thrown back in time. Somewhere between eight and ten hours. Someone should find him.'

He gave me a quizzical look. I responded by raising my finger to my lips. He knew what that meant. For the second time today, however, the device on my wrist betrayed me. 'Nice bracelet,' said the Doctor. 'It looks familiar.'

'Clever boy.'

'I suppose we have an appointment, then.'

'I suppose we do.'

'Can I offer you a lift?'

I shook my head. 'I have to tie up some loose ends of my own – but once that's done, we have a date. On Temple Beach.'

His face contorted in dismay. 'I didn't agree to that – will I?'

'I thought we'd skip that part, save time.' I smiled sweetly. 'Did I mention, it was a *really* huge favour?'

The Doctor looked up at the roiling sky. The electrical storm was still rumbling and flashing, full force. 'Oh, OK, fine,' he acceded, with bad grace, 'but I'll tell you now, I'm not wearing the thong – again.'

He turned to leave – and the pair of us froze in our tracks.

A figure had appeared at the car park entrance: a man in his mid-to-late forties, his shoulders slumped. He wore a crumpled grey suit and carried a battered brown leather briefcase. The Doctor frowned at him. 'Isn't that…?'

I hurried up to the new arrival. 'Martin Flint.'

He took my proffered hand, uncertainly, still trying to look past me at the monster slumbering on the cobbles. 'Um, yes, I… I'm here for an interview with Mr Smith, but I'm a few minutes late, there was a problem with—'

I slipped my arm around his shoulders. I steered him firmly around, back out onto the street. 'Martin, I'm afraid I have some bad news for you…'

So, this is how it happened in the end.

Martin Flint left his basement flat in the London suburbs at 10.45 a.m. He had to call in at his office for a couple of hours. That afternoon, he had an interview with a new but promising business based on Great Russell Street.

At the office, he received a phone call from his bank, telling him his account had been emptied. In a fluster, he left to deal with it.

I imagine that entailed a long meeting with his bank manager or customer services representative. No doubt, he was promised a thorough investigation. His life savings, however – almost £1500 – may have been gone for good.

No wonder he lost track of time!

He arrived for his interview late, and no one answered the door. He went around the back of the building, where he encountered a pair of strangers. They informed him that Dead Cert Investments had been unexpectedly liquidated. Martin's contact there – a Mr Smith – had left the country.

He also noticed a giant, green alien slug, sleeping in the car park. I expect he tried not to think too hard about that.

He had left his briefcase at work. Another shock was waiting for him when he went to collect it. A giant, green alien slug had threatened his co-workers, looking for him. More perplexing yet must have been said co-workers' insistence that Martin had been here shortly after the attack – and taken his case away with him.

By now, he must have wondered about his mental health.

Returning home, he found his flat in a terrible mess. The only things missing, though, were a few clothes from his wardrobe – in exchange for which a pair of striped hospital pyjamas were strewn across his bed.

Two men from the Unified Intelligence Taskforce were waiting to speak to him. He spent most of the evening trying to answer their questions, likely ending up none the wiser himself.

So, that was Thursday July the seventh 2016. A bright, warm summer's day with crystal-clear blue skies. A bad day for Martin Flint.

Friday was rather better.

On Friday morning, Martin found his briefcase sitting outside his front door. His missing shirt, suit trousers and socks were folded on top of it. His files of vital paperwork were undisturbed inside its compartments, alongside his phone – and something else. A betting slip, filled out in his own handwriting.

He handed the slip in at his local bookies, tentatively, fearing a hoax – and found himself some twenty thousand pounds richer. He had enough money to repair the damage to his flat and more beside.

You're right, Dear Diary, the Doctor probably wouldn't approve. On the other hand, who's ever going to tell him? Anyway, I happen to know he's scooped a few lottery jackpots himself. As I said – a real stickler for the rules, when it suits him.

Martin deserves that money.

He deserves it because, somewhere, some-when, another Martin Flint – and don't ask me where he came from, because there's no simple answer to that question – is trapped in a perpetual time loop.

Every day for him is Thursday July the seventh. Every morning, he wakes up shivering in a car park, his memory in shreds. Every afternoon, he stumbles into a rift in time, which sends him back to the start again.

Every day, he bets his life savings on a horse. Every day, he is snogged by a stranger outside his flat and attacked by a giant, green alien slug. Every day, he makes the bravest decision anyone could ever make.

And every day – every single day of his now-immortal life – Martin Flint saves the universe.

Death in New Venice
Guy Adams

1

You have to love Venice, it's the law.

Of course, it depends on the year. If you make the mistake of visiting during the late twentieth or early twenty-first centuries, you're going to have to squint a bit. The crowds, the floods, the corpulent tourists taking selfies with busking violinists... The Gondoliers, singing any old tosh in an Italian style to appease couples whose approach to romance is to throw money and cliché at it. (I once watched a Gondolier hammer out Tom Jones tunes, his face empty, his customers entranced, as if 'Delilah' might, perhaps, just *possibly* have been written by Verdi.)

These are the fast-food moments. The compromises. This is what happens when a place is forced to sell off a piece of its soul in order to keep the money rolling in. After all, you have to keep the lights on somehow.

But one of the main advantages to time travel is that you can shop around. Take the late fifteenth century, for example: it smells worse but it has class. It also has a fairly libertarian attitude (*love* a libertarian attitude). I mean, yes, after a lovely couple of days pottering I did end up being chased by the Doge's guards but, fair enough, I had broken into the palace, so they were only doing their job. But then, so was I, something I had to explain to Docherty on what seemed like a daily basis.

'Professor Song,' he'd say, 'please, just do your job.'

But we'll get to him later.

So, yes, I had to take a closer look at the Doge's Palace, because…

Well, we'll get to that later.

Anyway, I was having a fine old time, mooching around the corridors, eyeing up the paintings, having a cheeky tasting in the wine cellars, all in the name of honest research. And yes, I'll admit getting caught in the Doge's bedroom was awkward for all concerned, but I simply had to try his sheets and, give me some credit, I've done worse, at least the Doge wasn't in the room at the time. And yes, trying to gather up my clothes while soldiers were waving swords at me was something of an irritation (but you simply don't appreciate good cotton unless you feel it next to your skin). And yes, I do think the Captain of the Guard was overreacting a bit when he tried to brain me with a decorative axe but, live and let live, it was a startling five minutes for all of us and I'm sure he's probably an absolute poppet when not being thrown through the air by a partially clothed woman.

I kept my calm and didn't let the situation distract me from my research. I even took the time to appreciate and memorise the delightful stained-glass window that looked out over the Grand Canal. I'll admit I did then smash it with the aforementioned decorative axe but when a girl needs an exit she does what she must. There was a simply spectacular sunset that evening, I noticed as I let gravity have its wicked way with me. I remember thinking more people should be looking at it but then, I suppose, a woman flying through the air can be quite distracting.

There is only one truly acceptable perspective from which to appreciate the Grand Canal: being on the *outside* of it. I have showered four times since that dive and still smell of all the things you wouldn't want to smell of that can be found in canals. It's moments like this that make me wonder if DreamInc are paying me enough.

DreamInc, yes, let's talk about them a little, shall we? After all, everyone else does. Set up in the late twenty-seventh century (Earth Standard) by a pair of benign young space hippies, all Quinoa and beards, it was supposed to be the ethical, socially conscious travel company. Low eco-impact holidays for the overpaid professional who wanted an extra side order of smug with their vacation. It was sweet, in its own way, and I have no doubt that its original founders meant well, right up until they were offered an amount of money for the company that would rival most planets' GDP. At that point they shaved off the beards, banked the cash and retired to a particularly shiny corner of the universe to spend it in exciting, exhausting ways.

The current owner of the company is a corporation run out of Krellane, that damp, crustacean-packed planet most famous for its arms manufacture. Which, you know, is life and I'm not going to add to the considerable journalistic backlash that already exists. Hippies sell out, money talks. *Plus ça change…*

Besides, they're my current employers, and Section 87, Paragraph 112 of my contract stipulates that if I so much as raise a sardonic eyebrow as to the integrity of the company I'm in breach of terms and, as much as I love raising eyebrows, sardonically or otherwise, I'm not going to blow four million credits on it, even here in a private diary.

Luckily my contract makes no such stipulation when it comes to discussing the company's employees so let me state for the record: the DreamInc Executive Manager I've been dealing with, Milton Docherty, is a creep, and merely glancing at him makes my reproductive organs hide to the left of my kidneys for fear I might accidentally allow his DNA to propagate. This would never happen, they should trust me, but I can understand their refusal to take unnecessary risks.

At some point, someone once told him that a ponytail was attractive, possibly as a joke. Failing to see the funny side, he's had one transplanted and the result coils around his neck in a way that would only be acceptable were it throttling him.

He wears suits made from that horrendous Strackian silk that changes colour in order to complement its surroundings. As he's currently spending much of his time on a building site this means he's wandering around wearing a half a million credit bag of cement.

He has two ways of shaking people's hands. If you're a man he attacks you, desperate to prove how strong his grip is. If you're a woman he lingers, as if hoping you forgot to compile your body correctly that morning and you've accidentally put a far fruitier part of yourself where your palms ought to be.

Basically: he's just awful.

Perhaps I'm being unfair, there must be something good I can say about him. Oh yes, he had the good sense to employ *me*. Maybe he just likes shaking my hand.

He's working on the final stages of DreamInc's new business venture, an exclusive housing project called New Venice. When finished (which it will be in a matter of a few weeks) it will be a gated planetary community aimed at the sort of people who are so rich they'll barely bother to live there, just as they don't in all of their other exclusive homes. A half-empty, shiny collection of houses so technologically advanced they're only a couple of nudges away from sentience. It will be horrible, but being employed to help design it will have paid my bills for the foreseeable future so I care not one jot. I am not an arbiter of Universal good taste, let them do what they want.

DreamInc's trump card is a new invention called WishCrete (oh how I wish they'd stop smooshing words together, it's only charming when you're German). It's… hang on… where's the brochure…? 'An innovation in psychic-active construction technology, an amorphous and pliable building substance initially programmable through focused mental input which will continue to shift long-term as it reflects the desires and thoughts of those in proximity with it.' Which is a rather overblown way of saying you think it into shape. A house that can alter its structure depending on its residents' desires. Because that can't possibly go wrong, can it? I look forward to the first domestic argument here at New Venice and the resultant press release that explains precisely why a kitchen beating its inhabitants to a pulp wasn't the legal responsibility of DreamInc.

The WishCrete is also where I come in and why I've been having so many jolly trips to Venice through the ages, soaking up the atmosphere in general and the architecture in particular. Every morning I'm wired up to the WishCrete central programming hub and what I've learned is absorbed into its core structure. Of course, DreamInc don't know that I'm getting my information by actually going to Venice, they just think I'm terribly clever and well-informed. Which I am, so should this diary fall into their hands I'd also like to point out that, under Section 34, Paragraph 17, how I go about my research is my business and they can't fire me for it.

On the subject of which, time for me to go and plug in for an hour (any longer and the mental upload provides more information than the WishCrete can process). Nice work if you can get it.

2

Well, that was an interesting morning. And you know that, when I say 'interesting', I mean, 'Oh lord, that's a bit worrying.'

I did my usual upload (paying particular attention to Gothic arches) and then popped over to the canteen for a spot of breakfast. They do a very lovely vat-grown bacon roll (all the pig, none of the guilt) and their coffee is strong enough to defend itself against even the most aggressive palate. I've been chatting on and off to Gloriana, the site construction manager. Her putdowns are hammer blows and her tongue is hacksaw sharp. I once watched her make a lascivious steelworker cry after he made the mistake of hitting on her in the site bar. One look and he was begging for mercy.

'This is not a good day,' she told me as I sat down with my faux bacon and coffee. 'I would like this day to be shot for crimes against me.'

'What's up?' I asked her.

'One of the crews assigned to the east quarter is refusing to work. Union's backing them under the "clear and present danger" clause of their contracts.'

'What's the danger?'

She looked me right in the eyes (stealing a piece of bacon with her left hand, thinking I wouldn't notice, the minx) and said: 'Ghosts.'

'Ghosts?'

'Ghosts.'

Now, this is the sort of thing that requires explanation and I was sure Gloriana would get around to it just as soon as she'd finished chewing the bacon she'd stolen from me.

'It's not the first time someone claims to have seen something,' she said. 'In fact it's been site-wide gossip for the last week or so, ever since one of the workers spotted a woman dancing in the bedroom of the house he was working in.'

'How did he know she was a ghost?'

'They haven't put the floor in yet.'

'Nice moves.'

'I know, right? He ran out of there telling everyone to come and look and, of course, by the time they did, there was nothing there.' She took a sip of my coffee. 'The guy's got a bit of a history with drink so, to begin with, nobody was taking it seriously. Then he upped and left, walked out on his contract because he was too scared to go back in the house. People took him a bit more seriously after that.'

I bet they did. To limit industrial espionage, any worker leaving the site before the completion date is subject to a mandatory mind wipe. Not only do you lose your wages but you lose several months of your life. It's not something you'd do on a whim. I said as much to Gloriana.

'According to a guy he'd made friends with, the mind wipe was one of the reasons he walked, said he couldn't wait to forget about what he saw.'

'A dancing woman? Doesn't seem that terrifying.'

Gloriana nodded. 'Apparently it wasn't just a one-off, though; he *kept* seeing her. He didn't talk about it

THE LEGENDS OF RIVER SONG

because he knew people didn't really believe him but, according to this mate of his, she turned up everywhere after that. In his bedroom while he was sleeping, in the middle of the street, in the damn shower… He said she wouldn't leave him alone.'

'Do we know if he's seen her since?'

She shook her head. 'Company policy, no contact. Right now he doesn't even know he ever worked for DreamInc so none of their people are going to blow that fact by talking to him.'

I finished my coffee before she could do it for me. 'OK, so that's just one man, what about the rest?'

'That's where it gets really freaky. You know what stories are like. After the first guy left, the whole thing turned from being a joke to being something people took seriously. Within twenty-four hours, nobody was admitting they'd ever laughed about it. It was a *fact*. New Venice was haunted. Problem is, looks like they're right.'

Here's what she told me. (I haven't got time for all this damn dialogue, besides I'm paraphrasing like hell, if I could really remember what she said, word for word, my memory would be so brilliant I wouldn't need a diary.)

Next door to the dancing woman we had a small group of children running through the walls. They were seen by an entire work crew, all of whom downed tools and went running as if their souls depended on it (straight to the site bar, naturally).

Then there was an old woman sat in an, as yet unplumbed, bath who appeared to be crocheting. She was seen by someone with a bit more grit. He approached her and tried to touch her. At which point she deposited her crochet needle in his arm and screamed with laughter. By the time he had run to the medical station there was no longer any sign of the needle itself; it had vanished en route. The wound was real enough, though, and bleeding profusely. The doctor claimed said wound was psychosomatic; the man with a limb that was dripping on his shoes said he didn't care as long as the damn thing got stitches.

This upped the ante of the hauntings. Seeing something weird was one thing, being stabbed by it quite another. The east-quarter workers got together and agreed that none of them were happy working on a site where dead women might attack them.

Gloriana was now caught in the middle. DreamInc were demanding she got her crews back to work and the unions were insisting that wasn't going to happen, not until steps were taken to ensure the site was safe. But how did you make a site safe against ghosts? This was a question Docherty was clearly considering when I walked past him on my way back here.

'How much to get a priest here on high-speed shuttle?' he was shouting into his satphone. 'What sort of priest? What do I know? A cheap one!'

Things could be getting interesting.

3

Well, I've had one hell of an afternoon escaping the advances of a lustful baker in 1846. We've all been there. Never compliment a man on his focaccia unless you're absolutely sure he hasn't been single for five years. My trousers are so covered in flour you could bake them into a leg pie.

At least it got me off-site for a bit. Since I last updated the diary, things have taken a turn for the worse.

Docherty got his priest, a rather confused-looking man who claimed to be a representative of the Universal Union of Combined Faiths (business card motto: 'No matter your deity, we've got you covered'). He wandered the east quarter for a morning, chanted a bit, doused a few brick walls with 'holy spirit', a pungent concoction that smelled like the sort of thing you'd enjoy drinking right up until you went blind and couldn't find the plastic bottle it came in any more, and then presented his invoice.

'This building site is clean,' he announced and was about to rubber stamp the walls of the buildings when a DreamInc rep stopped him.

Despite the absurdity of it all, the union agreed (with the extra sweetener of a 0.5 per cent wage increase) to return to work. A few days of construction later, tools were downed once again. Someone else had been attacked and this time it was more serious than a crochet needle in the arm.

Jared Chadwick, one of the onsite architects, had been checking the angles on an underwater terrace designed to accommodate aquatic residents. According to Klepki, a Fractalian marine biologist who was working nearby (they've been gene-splicing koi carp to act as drinks vendors to the terrace visitors… I *know*) he was attacked by a figure wearing 'some sort of weird mask'. After Klepki did a sketch, Clever Old Me can confirm the attacker was dressed as the Arlecchino commedia dell'arte character (or Harlequin if you're not as clever and classy as me, which you probably are because I'm the only one allowed to read this diary).

The figure appeared from out of one of the seaweed displays and promptly choked the architect. When Klepki was asked why s/he didn't help, s/he pointed out that their species were devoutly against physical contact with gender-binary species and to intercede would have gone against centuries of cultural belief. Thanks for that, Klepki; I'm sure the dead man (and, indeed, his grieving family) quite understand.

(I know, I'm sounding bigoted. I'm just cross. I'll try and say something nice to a Fractalian at some point down the line in order to atone, but not just now. Just now I'm too livid.)

A few scared workers is one thing, a fatality is another. I decided I should talk to Docherty and get an idea as to what DreamInc planned to do about it.

'Get your damn hands off me, woman!' was his measured reply. I suppose I did go in guns blazing. You know me.

'Accidents happen on construction sites all the time,' he insisted, after I'd apologised and promised to cover the cost of repairing his ponytail implant. 'We can't just draw a halt to work because of one unfortunate incident.'

I don't know why I was surprised. The grand opening is only a fortnight away and a late opening will cost DreamInc the sort of money normal sentient beings can't write down numerically without getting bored with all the zeroes. Every day late is a financial apocalypse. It's the sort of money that's so large it's arguably not real any more, theoretical economics, but it carries weight with people like DreamInc and Docherty. In fact it's the only thing that does. Arguing against it is just raging against the wind.

I think even the workers understand that. I give it an afternoon before they're back at work.

4

Chatted to Gloriana again. She looks like she's forgotten what sleep is.

As predicted, DreamInc have thrown money at the union. Their contracts always included a default penalty should work not be completed on time and, while the unions were trying to plead extenuating circumstances, there's no legal precedent for ghosts causing problems on construction sites so that hasn't helped their negotiations. DreamInc have drawn a line in the sand as far as completion is concerned, softening the clenched fist with the addition of a hefty bonus, reliant on schedule. Basically: 'No, you can't have any more time but we'll pay you a lot of lovely extra cash if you just stop arguing and get on with it.'

The union have accepted. Money talks on every level. The workers need the pay and the bonus is large enough that even the loudest complainants can currently be found swinging hammers like it's a matter of life or death.

Let's hope it's not.

5

Gloriana turned up drunk at my apartment. Which is just the sort of fun thing I normally relish but I was halfway through trying to wash a bucket of pig entrails out of my hair so I wasn't in the most receptive mood.

(The pig entrails were an accident, and the Venetian butcher was terribly apologetic… I think. It was hard to hear him clearly with the bucket on his head.)

I stuck Gloriana in the living room to drown herself in coffee while I untangled a piece of porcine lung from my fringe. By the time I was in a fit state for visitors she'd passed out behind the sofa so I left her a note saying I'd be back in a bit and popped off to do my hour's upload.

Have I told you about the upload? Why am I asking you? YOU'RE A BOOK.

(A brilliant one written by a genius.)

This is how it works:

The central programming hub is a surprisingly small room beneath New Venice. (All of the maintenance areas are underground; rich people don't like seeing behind the scenes, they prefer to think the lights stay on by magic.) It's run by Viola, a sweet if slightly strange woman who is clearly terrified of people. She has that nervous twitch found only in the habitual Infonet user. To her, people should be lines of text on a forum page, emotions expressed by gifs, not something so raw and terrifying as a facial expression. In real life, smiles are just something filled with teeth. She's got used to me by now, of course, less likely to hide behind the upload array and occasionally even makes eye contact.

I've had fibre ports surgically installed, which freaked me out just enough to add another decimal point to my bill but are actually no big deal. The neural cabling is so thin it's like having a spray of high-tech acne at the base of your skull. I'll probably keep them; wetware's pricey so it's a bit of a bonus having them installed at no charge.

(Another advantage of time travel is that your gadgets never date unless you want them to. If I had to exist in a linear universe, six months of technological advancement would render these implants the equivalent of having a gramophone dumped in my cerebellum. As it is, I can plunder this moment of being cutting edge to my heart's content.)

Viola, after laughing nervously at nothing for a bit, wires me up and gives me a drink of something foul and salty that's supposed to boost the electrical charge in my body. The synapses, now given a bit of extra fizz, make better connections and upload speed is improved. For half an hour afterwards my hair will be dancing of its own accord and I'll be getting static shocks off everything I touch.

Now plugged in, Viola flips a switch and the connection between my brain and the WishCrete is open. It's like having the heavy weight of drunkenness draped over you instantly without all that fun time spent drinking fruity liquids. It's like a chainmail duvet plonked on your face.

Once the site is open, the WishCrete will operate directly with the residents and without all of this intimacy but then its response will be more vague. It will respond only to particularly strong emotions, and not (they hope) in such a profound, dramatic fashion. When I think of Venice, those thoughts are transmitted through the implants, the very soul of the place then written through the fabric of the WishCrete like the name of an awful seaside town through sweet rock. Not just the architecture, the cold but beautiful maths of arches and courtyards, but the *feel* of the place, the spirit of every street and water-lapped brick. New Venice will have its mother's heart.

That's why, in every session, while I do focus on specific details, individual buildings and streets, I also try and immerse myself in the atmosphere of Venice. I try and tell the WishCrete what it is to actually be there. You might think such subtle distinctions would be beyond such new technology, but walking through the newly minted walkways and sailing along the chemically safe canals it's honestly not bad at all. I'd go as far as to call it quite nice, in fact.

There are only two things that would stop me from living in New Venice once it's built: I couldn't afford it, and I'd hate to be trapped here with those few who could.

The whole business is painless. The only side effect seems to be a kind of dreaminess, a sense of disconnection from reality that lasts about as long as the static charge. I'll be wandering home with my head in the clouds, feet feeling like they're a hair's breadth above the ground.

When I finish, Viola gives me a saline wipe to swab away at the connections and another horrible drink, this one sweet enough to make your teeth shiver. It's disgusting but it sweeps up after a hangover like nobody's business, so today I took a bottle to give Gloriana on my return, knowing she'd love me for it.

She did. In fact by the time she'd gagged her way through a glassful she was almost human and I no longer had to worry about the possible fate of the carpets.

'Fun morning?' I asked her.

'It's morning?'

The night before had seen the worst accident yet, and the ghost sightings had spread from the east quarter. A team had been working on the recreation of Piazza San Marco, working alongside the morphing WishCrete to ensure the street lamps had the right aged look. One of the cybernetic wranglers had been releasing the automated pigeons to perch on the rooftops when they'd turned on him. It turned out to have been software failure rather than anything spooky but that was little consolation to him as he was pulled into beak-sized chunks and sprinkled over the Grand Canal.

The rest of the team had panicked and then, in the chaos, the bigger disaster had struck: the square flooded. Water crashed, seemingly from nowhere, and whisked the entire crew around the square. The only reason Gloriana was safe was that she'd been dangling from a lamppost at the time, trying to fix a faulty gas-replication jet. She hung there, clinging to the iron like a bear on a tree, watching as the dirty water slammed her men from one side of the square to another. While many of them had tried to swim clear, the tide was too strong and they were flung helplessly in whatever direction the water chose.

The whole thing lasted four minutes, then the water vanished as impossibly as it had first appeared. Everything was dry, the only sign of the flood were the bodies of thirty-two construction workers, scattered across the stone like driftwood, dry but puffy, shocked faces pressed into the ground. Some were lodged in railings or windows, some swept into the canal itself where they floated face down amongst the sprinkled remains of the cybernetic wrangler, bobbing up and down on the false tide caused by the underwater wave machines.

The waterways team have sworn the situation was nothing to do with them (and the fact that the water vanished leaving everything bone dry rather backs them up). DreamInc refuses to accept their assurances, mainly because the only other explanation is that a whole crew died by a ghost of a flood and even the union is terrified to accept *that* as a concept. Rationality is funny. People will accept a ghost if it's a mad knitter but not if it's an entire flood. As if scale makes all the difference.

Not that I'm saying it was a ghost in the traditional sense of course, because I'm a rationalist too, but one who has seen enough of the universe to roll with the punches. Whatever this is that's happening – and let's be honest it's not difficult to piece together – it needs addressing not denying. Of course, nobody wants to do it.

Except me.

6

'You need to deactivate the WishCrete.'

Docherty looked at me as if I'd gone mad. Actually, *madder*. I'm pretty sure he already thinks I'm mad anyway.

'WishCrete cannot simply be deactivated, Professor Song. It's psychic-active properties are baked into its very fabric. It's also one of the main draws to the future inhabitants of New Venice, a feature that they are paying considerably for. So tell me, why would I want to turn it into bog-standard concrete?'

'Because it's obviously killing people.'

I couldn't believe I was having to explain this.

'"Obviously"… That's an interesting use of the word.'

'People are seeing things,' I said. 'Images coming out of thin air around them. These images are causing psychosomatic injuries and death. If only there were an explanation, here in this building site packed full of a psychic-active substance that we know can shift and alter the surroundings based on the mental input of others.'

'You really think people are imagining themselves dead?' he asked. 'How does that make sense?'

'People don't just imagine *good* things you know,' I told him. 'Trust me, I'm looking at you this very minute and what I'm imagining happening to you is not, by any definition of the word, *nice*.'

He was about to say something he'd regret so I took pity on him and stopped him by carrying on speaking:

'Say the first sighting was actually a mistake. The man who saw the woman dancing. Maybe he was delusional, maybe he *was* drunk. But once he talked about it, the story spread, the concept grew. People began to think the place was haunted and that they'd see ghosts. Their expectation becomes reality thanks to the properties of WishCrete. It picks up on it, alters New Venice to fit people's expectations. *It does its job.*

'Then somebody wonders if these "ghosts" can actually hurt them. Lo and behold, no sooner has that idea been thought it becomes a reality. But wait, thinks the next person... If it can hurt, maybe it can *kill*... And *boom*, now it can. The WishCrete is constantly reflecting the dominant thoughts of everyone here. You've created a substance that responds to mental stimuli; it's not capable of distinguishing good thoughts from bad. You start being convinced something awful is going to happen and it's happy to oblige.'

I let him get a word in, just to show willing.

'So you're saying it's only happening because the working crews think it's going to? That doesn't make the remotest sense. You think someone out there decided the square was going to flood so it did?'

'The square used to flood all the time,' I explained (though in truth not in quite such a dramatic manner, though he wouldn't know that any more than the workers who had been onsite at the time). 'All it took was one person to think about that. "Just imagine," they think, "what it would be like if you were stood here and this whole place flooded." The minute that thought's out there…'

'Rubbish,' he said, proving how pointless that entire conversation was.

7

I talked to Gloriana today about my theory. Unlike Docherty, she didn't argue with a word of it. Of course she didn't – she has a fully functioning brain.

Not that it matters. The 'accident' in the square has been blamed on the waterways team, the head of which has been fired and construction continues regardless. New Venice opens in five days, and DreamInc has no intention of letting anything as annoying as a potentially catastrophic design error get in the way of the fact.

I've got two choices, presented to me succinctly by Docherty:

1. I leave now, defaulting on my contract and incurring the financial penalties of that. (Like I care. Unlike some, I'm not so cold as to trade off the health of my bank balance against the loss of innocent life.) I will also receive the contracted mind wipe. Which means I won't know about any of this. It'll play out without my involvement.

2. I retain my position and shut my mouth (otherwise I'll be fired, see option one).

What choice have I got? If I leave here, voluntarily or otherwise, it won't save any lives. This whole mess will just become something I later read about in one of the news feeds, not knowing I might have been able to help.

If I stay, pretend to be a good girl, I might be able to do something.

Might.

How I hate my life sometimes.

8

Two days to the grand opening. I actually had a fashion team visit the house and measure me for a frock. I suggested it be made in pine with brass handles but the joke went over their heads somewhat.

DreamInc has a whole events team in place, charged with recreating a Venetian Grand Carnival, fancy dress, parades, masked balls, fireworks, just the sort of thing that goes down a storm with a bit of mass slaughter.

All of the housing plots are sold, their owners being ferried in between now and then. DreamInc have tried to keep people out right up until the last minute but even they can't win an argument with customers capable of buying out their entire genetic line and having it scrubbed. So a few people have moved in already.

I saw a ridiculously ostentatious speedboat belting up and down one of the canals this morning. It was driven by a child, screaming her enthusiasm with every wave. Just for a second I found myself wondering what might happen if she bounced too high and hit her head on one of the low bridges. I had to stop myself. If I was right – and I am – I could have *made* it happen. One stray thought and a bridge could have squatted down and clipped her off above the neck as I watched.

A Romanadi couple have moved in up the road from my apartment, I can see them now. He's stood on his balcony, looking at the view while inside his husband is arguing with a drinks mixer. Apparently the vodka isn't cold enough. Poor poppet.

I've now closed my window before I think anything too uncharitable in their direction.

Two days. Two days and then this place will be full.

I think the panic of the deadline has focused people actually. Determined to get their bonuses, wishing everything would just go right, no more mistakes, no more delays, just a clean, perfect build. There have been no more accidents. Hooray for the power of positive thought. Once everyone's turned up that'll change. That tunnel vision will widen out and who knows what will happen? Nothing good, unless I can think of a way to stop it, which, right now, I can't.

9

Gloriana's gone. Apparently she was shipped out in the night after getting into a bust-up with Docherty. She couldn't stand by and let this happen so she kicked up a fuss and is now lying in a medical centre somewhere, post-mind wipe, wondering what she's been up to for the last six months.

Gloriana was disposable.

I know Docherty wants to keep me around; I'm something else to waft in front of his rich clients. I'm the highly regarded (shush) expert DreamInc hired at great cost to get everything right. I'm to be shown off like a gilt tap or a particularly breathtaking water feature. He actually asked me to make a speech at the opening ceremony. I told him not to push his luck.

Gloriana was just an employee. Firing her has saved them money and he'll have done it with a smile, the odious toad.

I've taken a look at my contract and the minute the place opens the particularly troubling clauses evaporate into air. Effectively, my employment with DreamInc stops the minute the doors officially open. After that, they can't fire me, mind wipe me or threaten me in any way. I'll be free.

One day to go.

10

The opening ceremony.

Sigh…

Nobody died, let me make that quite clear. Though the day is young, so don't breathe out just yet. I'm taking a breather in nineteenth-century Florence because I just had to get out of there for a minute. (Another advantage of time travel: when you really need some space you can put down your champagne, walk off for five years and then go straight back before your drink's so much as lost its chill.)

I suppose it was impressive, if you've never seen a Fellini movie. The canal was filled with huge, decorative, floating grotesques. Barges designed to look like fish, fireworks erupting from their gills at every opportunity. Those residents not already in situ were inside them, ferried from the spaceport to the main island. The barges were moored up alongside the Rialto Bridge and shoals of mechanised fish filled the water so that the passengers could walk to dry land on their softly carpeted backs. Once ashore, the pampered residents were on dry land for all of five minutes, presented with their welcome packs (which included, I kid you not, a complimentary boat), their carnival costumes and their house keys, and then dumped back on the canal again as they were taken on a gondola ride around the city.

I had tried to avoid that but Docherty made it clear I was to join an aged couple who had specifically asked to meet me. As New Venice wasn't officially declared open for another hour, I had little choice but to clamber on board and put on my very best fake smile.

Quite *why* the couple wanted to meet me was never entirely clear. They certainly never asked anything about me. They had made their money salt mining the Prentiss Cluster and took every opportunity to mention the fact.

'People always want salt,' the wife said, while readjusting her beauty spot from one cheek to another, 'as I told darling Ludovic when we first met.'

Darling Ludovic didn't say much, just stared at my chest and tried to stop his jodhpurs riding up to expose his surgically repaired knees. I think Darling Ludovic lives in fear of his wife, as well he might.

'I suppose this place is acceptable,' she said, tearing her eyes away from her make-up mirror for a couple of seconds. 'I just hope it's secure.'

You and me both, I thought. 'The security protocols at the spaceport are terribly strict,' I assured her. 'You can't even land here if your bank balance isn't large enough.'

'Quite right,' she said, adding another dollop of foundation. 'People don't understand how we *suffer*. It's such a burden being wealthy, simply everyone wants a piece of you. Darling Ludovic is constantly besieged. People resent it, you see. The universe does so hate success, and the proles will try and tear you down. You ask anyone.'

I checked my watch. Still forty-five minutes before I could be honest.

'It must be awful,' I said.

'It is,' she nodded. 'I just hope we've finally found somewhere where we can relax.'

I really had nothing to say to that.

Gondola trip done, everyone was gathered in Piazza San Marco (with all of the staff pretending very hard that more than thirty people hadn't died there a few days ago). More fireworks were lit, champagne corks popped and, with a longwinded speech that tested the endurance of all in attendance, Docherty declared New Venice open.

At which point I ran away, no longer employed, to have a bit of a think.

It's the old rich woman in the gondola I keep returning to in my mind, realising that all rich people think the same way: 'The proles will try and tear you down.'

That is not a thought she wants to have in New Venice because, sooner or later, it will prove her right.

11

It was sooner.

I dropped back in on New Venice about five minutes after I'd left and the screaming had already started.

The opening ceremony had been the cue to commence the carnival, the streets filling with a laid-on procession that the new residents would now join, making their way through the city and returning to the square, by which time it would have been laid up for a banquet with some godawful Croxian Opera offered up as pudding.

They didn't get that far.

The procession arrived in the square and, at its head was the Arlecchino, immediately recognised by the Fractalian who, despite their discomfort at being around binary-gendered life forms, was, by all accounts, having a simply marvellous time with a bottle of French brandy.

The events manager, a wonderfully shrill octopod with a determination to make the word 'frabjous' cool by repeating it endlessly, was understandably confused. She hadn't booked that many revellers in the procession, just a handful of android performers designed to get the party mood started. Staring at the endless ranks flooding into the square, twirling their banners and dancing along the cobbles she was heard to say, 'That's *so* not frabjous' before the bloodletting began.

The first to fall was a young man from Alcapha who, I'm informed was a famous pop star in his galaxy. The man behind such golden hits as (translated into English) 'Girl, That's My Pseudopod You're Holding' and 'Maybe We Should Just Make Eggs'. Perhaps encouraged by the sound of the marching band, he leaped into the procession and began dancing lasciviously with a woman in a feather headdress and layers and layers of silk and lace. She bit his head off.

Then came a trio dressed in the traditional Plague Doctor masks and black cloaks. Their long, ceramic noses were crimson with blood by the time they'd finished examining the entrails of their unwilling patients.

By the time a swarm of pigeons – not the repaired DreamInc variety but an ethereal, WishCrete creation – began to swoop on the crowds they were already running. Some tried to get back on the boats but the water itself had turned against them, great waves forming open hands that slapped people away or scooped them up and hurled them skywards. Others ran deeper into New Venice, funnelling themselves through the alleyways leading off the square, desperate to keep ahead of the homicidal revellers that were also dividing off and pursuing them.

Me? I was dangling off one of the palace balconies desperately screaming into my communicator.

'Gloriana! We need you now!'

OK, so maybe I need to go back a bit.

Before returning to New Venice I'd tracked down Gloriana. It wasn't hard: she was widely advertising her availability for work, her CV cluttering up most of the Employment Agency sales feeds from Earth to Galactic Centre. I'd offered her a job.

'Driving?' she'd said. 'I don't do driving. I'm a construction site manager.'

'I know that,' I assured her, 'but I'll make it worth your while.'

It seemed only right that she saw some kind of return on her time at New Venice.

I'd hired one of those huge settlement wagons. You know the kind of thing, designed for transplanting colonies, built like a small moon and loaded with the sort of short-range transmat technology that's terribly useful when landing your ship on a planet's surface is likely to crack it wide open.

You can imagine my relief then, as the sound of a couple of square miles of displaced air lets me know she's moving into the atmosphere above us.

'River?' Her voice comes through on the communicator. 'You want me to start gathering people up?'

'Lock on to every life sign you can and gather away.'

'On it. You know I can't do everyone at once?'

Even a settlement wagon has its limitations.

'Yeah, just grab people as quickly as you can.'

So, as the air started to fill with the sound of groups of people being transmatted to safety in the troposphere, I climbed into the palace and gave some thought as to how I could get to where I needed to be without dying.

Which is when I discovered that even the buildings bore a grudge.

The walls of the palace reached out to me as I ran towards the ground floor, giant brick fists that wanted to hammer me into paste against the marble and ancient stone. I was truly regretting my rather overblown new frock as I tried to move quickly through a never-ending attack of fixtures and fittings.

I ended up running along the Bridge of Sighs, so named, it's said, from when state prisoners would be marched across it, taking their one last look at freedom before incarceration in the prison on the other side.

I rechristened it en route. During its short lifespan it became the Bridge of Deliciously Inventive Biological Swears.

Perhaps it didn't approve, as it tried to kill me by detaching itself but, as you know, I was starting to make a habit of diving into that damn canal and it would seem that even the processing power of WishCrete had its limitations as I managed to swim to land before anything else tried to kill me.

Access to the maintenance sections was located via a lift in one of the waterbus stations. To get there I had to negotiate my way past a herd of masked revellers. They were wearing wide-beaked bauta masks, their fat, gold noses actually twitching as they turned their tricorn-hatted heads towards me.

I had no reason to hope these WishCrete constructions would care if I shot them – after all, they weren't flesh or blood – but I cranked my gun to its highest setting, hoping I could at least cause enough damage to their structure to get past them.

I blew holes out of them as I ran past, their arms liquefying and reaching out to grab me even as I opened their bodies to the air. One of them caught me by the back of my frock but I managed to sever it at the wrist with a shot that also gave me an unwanted haircut.

I was beating off the crawling hand even as I made it to the waterbus stop and inputted my security code for the lift. Always did have a problem with wandering hands.

The lift arrived and, at least for now, I was away from the WishCrete. The maintenance areas were traditional build. WishCrete was expensive (and what value!) and there was no need to construct them with anything but normal materials.

Arriving on the underground level, who should I meet but Docherty.

'Professor Song! What a relief to see you're all right!' He made a fair fist of sounding sincere, but I wasn't interested; a good deal of the slaughter going on above us was his responsibility to bear.

'I thought I should see if I could help down here,' he said, before realising he wasn't creative enough to extend the lie further. There was nothing he could achieve down here because, unlike me, he wasn't built to do what needed to be done.

'How public spirited of you,' I said as we made our way towards the WishCrete central programming hub. 'You can help me if you like.'

'You've got a plan?'

'Oh yes… but first, we need to come to an agreement.'

Even in his panic, his eyes narrowed at that. You could threaten this man with any form of violent death but poke a finger towards his wallet and then you'd see real terror.

'I've employed someone to get as many of the people, including us, to safety as possible.'

'Wonderful.'

'It's cost me a fortune. How about you take this opportunity to take the credit and also cover my costs?'

'What sort of costs are we talking about?'

I told him. He blanched somewhat, and I'm not surprised as I'd doubled my actual expenses so as to build a sizeable pay-out for myself and Gloriana into the equation.

'I'd have to think that over,' he said, breaking out in a cold sweat.

'No time for that, I'm afraid. Here's how it's going to work: today could put DreamInc out of business. Just imagine how many people will be trying to sue in about an hour's time. But if you can convince everyone that plans to get them to safety and deal with the WishCrete problem were yours and already in place, you could come out of all this with a chance of saving your career, even if DreamInc sinks. Just think of all the rich people you'll be able to say owe their continued existence to your quick thinking.'

He thought about that for a moment and then nodded. 'What do I have to do?'

I gave him my bank codes and watched him tap away at his wrist computer as he authorised the transfer. When he was finished and the money sent, I told him to sit down in the corner and not get in my way. It really was the only useful thing I could think of for him to do.

We'd reached the central programming hub by now and, inside, Viola was going spare.

'The whole array is going into meltdown!' she said. 'I don't know how to stop it.'

'Plug me in,' I told her. 'I'll see what I can do.'

That heavy sensation I described before, as the WishCrete made contact, was entirely different this time. While the WishCrete wasn't sentient, it was capable of thought in a limited fashion and the assault on its programming was giving it the technological version of a nervous breakdown. There were so many conflicting emotional inputs. Even as people were panicking they would be hoping to get away safely: a conflict right there. It's a sad fact that most people are inclined towards the negative. However much they may be looking at their horrible circumstances and desperately hoping they may survive them, their overriding belief will be that they won't. 'I'll probably die of this,' they think, their glass truly half empty. And with that, the conflict is resolved, the loudest voice selected, the WishCrete fulfils their expectations. It kills them, just as they believed it probably would.

But with so many minds, so many voices, the WishCrete was struggling.

It was fortunate that it was still attacking on a one-on-one basis; that bought us time. On the subject of which…

'Gloriana?' I asked, tearing my mind away from the WishCrete for a moment to speak into my communicator. 'How are we doing?'

'A couple more minutes and I'll have everyone,' she said.

A couple more minutes. A lot of people can die in two minutes.

'OK. I need you to hold off on any life signs immediately surrounding mine.'

'What?' Docherty wasn't happy about the sound of that,

'Just until I've done what I needed to do,' I told him. 'We'll be fine, it can't kill us down here anyway.'

'That's what *you* think,' said Viola, showing us security footage of the entrance to the maintenance level. The lift was opening and a wave of WishCrete was pouring out, channelling itself down the lift shaft and reforming into carnival revellers as it reached the corridor. As I watched, the leader of this awful band, the Arlecchino, looked up towards the camera. He bowed in a pantomime fashion, then his arm elongated and snatched the camera off the wall, killing the feed.

'We need to go now!' said Docherty. 'They'll be here in minutes!'

'Minutes is all we'll need,' I reassured him. 'I'm going back in.'

And I closed my eyes and tipped my thoughts back into the WishCrete. I was its chief source of knowledge, I insisted. I was the great designer, the person who had given it its essential form.

I could feel its reluctance. It couldn't tear itself away from the braying victims above, even as they were vanishing thanks to Gloriana. Perhaps it didn't want to, perhaps it had a little more sentience than I gave it credit for. Perhaps it was actually starting to enjoy itself.

Listen to me! I insisted. *Your prime directive is for historical accuracy. That is the one rule you mustn't break.* And it hadn't. Even when attacking, it was attacking as historical Venice, it was staying in character. *So there's one more thing you need to know about Venice, one more thing you need to do in order to maintain your accuracy…*

It was starting to pay attention. I guessed that Gloriana had probably got everyone above ground to safety now so my voice was coming through clearer. In the distance (at least it felt like the distance, even though, in reality, it was only feet away) I could hear the sound of someone banging on the door to the central programming room. The carnival had arrived. I was out of time.

Just do as you're told! I insisted, my final thought before dragging myself back into the real world and the sound of panicking.

'We're trapped!' Docherty was screaming, his back to the door even as it buckled around him.

'Gloriana?' I shouted into the radio. 'Are we clear?'

'Everyone but the three of you in that room,' she replied. 'Want me to bring you up?'

'Two seconds,' I told her, waving at Viola to unplug me from the array. The last thing I wanted was to transmat up with a chunk of cabling still in my skull.

'Quickly!' Docherty screamed as the door finally gave way behind him, sending him tumbling into the room. In the now open doorway Arlecchino walked in, his black and white masked head twitching from side to side, his white-gloved hands flitting in the air like circling doves.

'Clear!' said Viola.

'Now!' I told Gloriana and the air fizzed with the transmat as we left New Venice behind and found ourselves on the bridge of the settlement wagon.

'I thought you'd rather be up here than with the rest of them,' said Gloriana, turning away from the controls to face us. 'They're none too happy.'

'I don't blame them,' I said. 'Can you pick up video from the surface of New Venice?'

She nodded, tapped a few buttons and we watched on the screen as the city toppled, waves of water spuming around the ancient buildings.

'Oh my god,' said Docherty, his face turning white to see the sum total of trillions of credits and months of work vanish right in front of him. 'What did you do?'

'I gave the WishCrete one final order,' I explained. 'I told it an important historical detail I hadn't mentioned before: what happened to the original Venice.'

'What?' He just shook his head, unable to process the cost of what he was seeing.

'It sank,' I explained and went in search of a nice lie down and a drinks dispenser.

River of Time
Andrew Lane

The biggest issue a girl has with long-term incarceration on a remote and dismal prison planet is, I've found, the effect it has on her shoes.

I will admit, if pressed, that the food is awful as well, but there are a few planets, moons and space stations near this godforsakenly remote solar system that will deliver a decent takeaway, for an admittedly hefty price (which I usually book to the Governor's personal account without her knowing). Boredom can be a problem, but I've taken it as an opportunity rather than a drawback, and thrown myself into archaeological research. Long distance, of course, but with even with the obsolete holographic technology they have at Stormcage (so archaic it almost counts as an archaeological project in its own right) it's honestly almost like being on site watching the work being done. But not actually taking part, of course. Loneliness can also be a problem here, but the small arthropods that come out of the cracks in the walls at night to forage for food are very good listeners. Sometimes, I've noticed, they even talk back, although when that starts happening I know it's time for an excursion.

Which brings me back to the subject of shoes.

The dampness, the lack of decent closet space and something corrosive in the atmosphere at Stormcage means that anything apart from Wellington boots rots away pretty quickly – and I'm not wearing Wellington boots for any reason. When you have to use your shoe heels as tools for prising the access panels off the robotic warders then you tend to snap a lot of them as well. That's why, every few months, I have to escape from Stormcage to do some serious shopping. After all, a girl has to look her best, doesn't she? One never knows when one might get a visit from one's husband – except, of course, that one is in here in the first place for killing him. Except that nobody can quite remember who he was.

I have a lot of time to think, here at Stormcage. That may not, I have decided, be a good thing. Still, at least the arthropods and I have plenty to talk about.

The Governor is frantic to know how I keep getting out. She keeps losing her annual bonus because of my little escapades. It makes her irritable. I don't know why – I always come back in the end. I actually have a vortex manipulator which I use to get out, but they never find it when they search my cell. Of course they don't – I keep it slightly out of phase with this reality. The remote control that calls it when I need it is small enough that I can hide it inside a scan-worm that I had implanted in my body by a very nice surgeon some years ago. Whenever the Governor has her warders run a scanner over me, looking for things I might be hiding, the scan-worm burrows around my body, getting as far away from the scanning radiation as it can. It tickles, but I'm a giggler anyway, so nobody notices me acting strangely. Well, no stranger than a woman whose supposedly dead and yet strangely unidentified husband is getting younger while she's getting older generally acts, anyway.

I was all prepared this morning for a little trip out to Kanenda Station, which caters to the most exclusive of clients in this quadrant of the galaxy. I found where the scan-worm was hiding by the simple expedient of feeling all over for it. I don't know what it looked like I was doing to anyone that was watching on the security monitors, but I hope they were enjoying the show. I'd just located the worm and I was pressing the button in its centre section to call the vortex manipulator to this reality when the door slid open and three warders rushed in, followed by the Governor herself. The warders had laser guns and neuronic whips, and sensors covering most of the electromagnetic spectrum all over their visored helmets, like a mass of black spikes. The helmets were introduced so that I couldn't drug them with my lipstick, of course, but that's a whole different story. I've acquired a new shade of lipstick with a solvent in it that will eat through anything, but that's another different story.

So many stories, so little time. Isn't that the most perfect definition of life?

Anyway, just as the vortex manipulator materialised on my arm they grabbed me and pulled it off.

'You've chipped my nail varnish,' I protested to the nearest one.

'It's probably poisoned anyway,' the Governor snapped, hands on hips. She has good hair and a reasonable fashion sense, but the humidity here is playing havoc with her complexion. 'Were you going somewhere?'

'Not any more,' I sighed. 'Do you really have to spoil a girl's fun like this? What if I promised to pick out some really nice lingerie for you while I'm shopping?'

'Do you really think you can bribe me with frilly underwear?' she snapped.

'I can bribe anyone with frilly underwear,' I retorted. It's true – I can.

'The ironic thing is,' she said, smiling thinly, 'that you didn't even need to sneak out this time. I was just coming down to tell you that you're going on a little trip.'

'Oh, how fabulous!' I said, but inside I was concerned. I could count on the knuckles of one finger how many times I'd been officially allowed out of Stormcage since I'd arrived, and none of them were pleasant.

I was escorted by the warders up to the Governor's office, which is in a tower that has a panoramic view over the second-most desolate, murky, storm-wracked terrain I've ever seen. (The most desolate, murky, storm-wracked terrain I've ever seen was a place called Canvey Island, on a planet called Earth, in a time that the locals refer to as the 1970s, but that's another story as well.) I've suspected for a while that the tower is actually an escape ship that the Governor can use if there's ever a riot, and I do intend checking that out at some stage, but when I was pushed into her office I was more intrigued by the other person sitting in front of her desk. He had a briefcase by his side.

'Inmate 50243,' the Governor said (we're not on first-name terms, despite my frequent attempts at being friends), 'this is Professor Darin Forcade.'

'River Song,' I said, smiling my best smile and extending a hand. 'Also a Professor.'

'I know,' he said, rising and walking over to me. He was a burly man with a bushy beard that had streaks of grey in it. 'I was very impressed with your paper about the Racnoss ruins on Arcnoy Twelve.'

'I'm flattered,' I said as he bent and kissed the back of my hand. Old-fashioned courtesy – I've always been a sucker for that. And bow ties. 'Equally, I thought your work on the Osiran artefacts found on the remains of their orbital Möbius strip near Arcturus came to some very interesting conclusions. They were wrong, of course, but still very interesting. Wrong is so much more preferable to boring, don't you find?'

He smiled. 'I'd like to retain your services, Professor Song.'

I glanced at the Governor, then back at him. 'I'd love to help,' I said. 'Unfortunately my schedule is a little full at the moment with this tiresome "life sentence for murder" thing. You may have heard about it.'

I saw the Governor grimace out of the corner of my eye. Honestly, she should avoid expressions like that: she doesn't seem to have a good skin-care regime in place, and the constant dampness of Stormcage is making her look much older than she actually is. Unless she's three hundred years old, in which case she's looking remarkably good.

'I understand,' Professor Forcade said. 'But the organisation that runs this facility has granted me a certain amount of latitude. You're the acknowledged expert on the long-extinct precursor races to have evolved in the galaxy. I need your help.'

I felt like a small child at Christmas. 'You've found more precursor ruins! Ooh – tell me more! Where are they? Which race?'

Forcade raised his hands in a shushing gesture. 'There's time enough on the journey to brief you on everything we found, but you need to know that there's something... unusual... that's been uncovered at the site. Something that you're uniquely positioned to give an opinion on.'

He glanced over at the Governor. She shrugged, and he walked over to retrieve his briefcase. As he returned he pulled a square of comp-paper from it and shook it open. He handed it to me and stood there, holding his briefcase in front of him like a shield.

What the comp-paper showed was a looped recording lasting a few minutes of several people in dirty coveralls trying to get a door open without breaking anything. The door was metal, but old enough and tarnished enough that it looked like stone. The wall it was set in was featureless, but three things struck me. The first thing was that the door was about five times the size of the archaeologists trying to get it open. The second thing was that someone ought to design a more flattering set of work clothes for archaeologists than the standard beige coveralls they all wear. They must get a bulk discount, but frankly it's not worth it. The third thing was that, judging by the glyphs set into the frame of the door, this wasn't Gallifrey. That was a relief.

I don't know very much about Gallifrey – just the fact that it was home to one of the first civilisations ever to emerge into the galaxy, the legends about it being 'a planet beyond time' and the fact that my husband and the love of my life was born there, but I know, from those legends and from things that he has let slip, that if Gallifrey is ever found then bad things will happen. Fortunately, this wasn't it.

'What strikes you?' Forcade asked.

'The warders here, every few days,' I replied. The Governor coughed. 'But also the size of the door. There aren't many races ever to have evolved in the galaxy that size. It's bigger than the Racnoss!'

'It could just be a large door for ceremonial purposes,' he ventured. I knew he was testing me.

'No,' I corrected him, 'the race that used that door were huge. The control glyph that opens it is about eighteen feet above the floor.'

He frowned. 'Control glyph?'

'The symbol they would have touched to open the door. It's more worn than the rest of them.'

'They're millennia old,' he pointed out. 'They're all worn.'

'Yes, but there's one that's a touch more degraded than the others. Tell your team to push it inwards to release the door. Most precursor civilisations used geothermal energy from the planet's core to power their cities. Assuming the ceramic wiring is still intact, the doors will open and close right up to the moment the planet breaks apart, and given the fact that all the races from those times have gone that's only likely to happen due to natural gravitational stress.'

He nodded reluctantly. 'They did find it, but by accident.'

I love being right, but I didn't have time to revel in it. 'What was inside?' I asked eagerly.

'That's what I want to show you,' he replied. His gaze flickered towards the Governor. 'But not here. On the planet.'

The Governor couldn't hold herself back any more. 'What's so important about all this?' she demanded.

Professor Forcade glanced at me, and made a small motion with his hand, indicating I should answer.

'Before any of the races in the universe today evolved,' I answered in my best lecture hall voice, 'there were other races. Older races. Archaeologists call them "the precursors". They have all died out by now – some by the natural decay and senescence that afflicts any civilisation, but some because of a series of great clearances that occurred longer ago than anyone can remember.' I felt myself frown, as my old researches surfaced from the depths of my memory. I stopped frowning as quickly as I could. It's simply the worst thing for creating permanent lines. 'It is said that several races joined together in a coalition to fight against horrors far worse than anything we experience now. This coalition was led by a race from a mysterious planet known only as... Gallifrey.'

My fingers were crossed behind my back, but neither the Governor nor Professor Forcade noticed.

'"The Rulers of Time",' Forcade muttered. 'Or perhaps "the Lords of Time" – the records are unclear.'

'"Lords" is more accurate,' I said quietly, then louder I continued: 'Over an indeterminate amount of time they laid waste to the Racnoss, the Narlok and the Great Vampires, as well as other that we have no record of—'

'Great Vampires!' the Governor scoffed. 'What do you take me for – some kind of idiot?'

'Let's leave that for posterity to judge,' I said smoothly. 'The phrase "Great Vampires" is a loose translation based on several very old texts. You might prefer to think of them as massive humanoid creatures capable of sucking the life from an entire world, and turning its inhabitants into acolytes. Anyway, once these threats were cleared, the coalition fell apart, and the various races that made it up started to turn inwards and decay. They're all long gone now.' Behind my back I was crossing my impeccably manicured fingers again. The Time Lords weren't gone, of course – not all of them anyway – but I wasn't going to go into that now. I tapped the comp-paper. 'Based on these glyphs, I'd say that this planet was occupied by the Qwerm.'

'The Qwerm?' Forcade was looking at me wide-eyed.

'They were, from what I have been able to piece together, a race of philosophers who became through some strange set of circumstances the warrior arm of the coalition. Massive, six-legged, like enormous locusts the size of a large Edwardian steam locomotive, if you know what that is – and as an archaeologist you certainly should – with five separate and interlinked brains capable of rapid parallel tactical and strategic analysis.' I glanced over at the Governor, who was listening to all this in open-mouthed fascination. 'The interesting thing about the precursor races, by the way, was that they were generally much larger than races now. Certainly the Racnoss were very impressive, and the Great Vampires weren't called that because of their art and their music. Nobody knows why they evolved to be so big. I've seen theories suggesting that it has something to do with the fact that some universal physical constant has been slowly reducing with time, but nobody really knows.' I smiled at them. 'The old legends say that the river of time was narrower then, near the source of time, and so the things that swam in it seemed bigger by comparison, but that's just poetic licence. Only the Osirans were about our size.'

'And these mysterious Rulers of Time,' Forcade pointed out.

I rolled up the comp-paper and handed it back to him. 'So – have I passed the test? Do I get to see what's on the other side of this door?'

He nodded, but there was something guarded in his expression. Something that made me feel uncomfortable. 'Yes,' he said.

'Then let's go.'

He glanced from me to the Governor and back. 'Do you need to pack? Does she want to pack?' He seemed confused over who had the authority here. I thought that was quite sweet of him. Obviously, it was me, but he'd only just met me. He'll learn.

'It's OK,' I said. 'I keep a packed bag by my cell door, ready for whenever I want to pop out.'

I could hear the Governor's teeth grinding from ten feet away. She should get them checked out by a good orthodontist. I'll make sure I recommend one to her when I get back.

Professor Forcade's ship is not luxurious. In fact, it's anti-luxurious, if that is even a word. If it isn't, well, I think it should be. It's a battered P-shifter so old that it might just have seen service in the Time Lord campaigns against the Racnoss and the Great Vampires. Maybe he likes it because it is an antique, or perhaps, being an academic, he can't get funding for anything better. Whatever the reason, I spent most of the journey in my quarters trying to get comfortable on a lumpy mattress while he kept offering me cups of tea, perhaps out of guilt. Fortunately I always pack a bottle of champagne in my travel bag. It's dimensionally transcendental – the bottle, not the bag – and I've never managed to exhaust the very pleasant vintage inside. It never warms up or loses its fizz either. There's probably a thousand years of technological development behind its design, but I don't particularly care about that – I just care that it works. It was the nicest present I have ever received.

I've been going over what little I know about those early Time Lord campaigns. I know that it took them a long time to lever themselves out of their torpor of complacency and initiate the Time War against the Dalek Empire, but back when they were a young race they were a lot more active and a lot more moral ('moral' being a relative term for whatever someone believes is right and are willing to fight for). And they were a lot more willing to get their hands dirty by working with other races. I imagine them as being then a whole race made up of people just like my husband.

The funny thing is that although I know quite a bit about their enemies back then, I don't know very much about any of the races they were working with apart from the Qwerm. I've seen passing references in obscure histories to a race called the Minyans and a planet called Karn, but that's about it. Were the other races in the coalition of the same standing as the Time Lords, or were they just cannon fodder, taken along for the ride? I wish I knew, and the only person I know who does know isn't talking. Well, actually you can't stop him from talking, but he rarely actually says anything.

I've also been wondering about this thing that the Professor wants me to look at – the reason why he came specifically to get me. My self-esteem is high enough that I could power a small world with it for several years, but even I don't think that my fame as an archaeologist is galaxy-wide. So how did Forcade come to pick me?

We arrived at the unnamed planet earlier today. From orbit it looks dusty, like something that's been left on the shelf for a long time. The sun is shrunken and blue, and gives off a harsh, cold light. Even from orbit I could see the partially erased geometry of ancient and decaying cities linked by vast highways and power grids. The Qwerm, being a large race themselves, built big and built to last, but as we came in to land in a huge plaza in the middle of an enormous city I could see that most of the walkways linking the enormous buildings – wide enough and thick enough to support the bodies of the huge, insectoid Qwerm – were broken. Fragments lay in the wide boulevards. The monolithic white buildings themselves were largely intact, but their huge windows had broken long ago, leaving oval holes that seemed to stare at us like thousands of dark eyes. There was no colour anywhere to soften the white of the buildings, the grey of the sky and the black of the weeds, as thick around as the Qwerm themselves, which had grown out of cracks in the ground and spiralled around the towers and the jagged remnants of the walkways.

Professor Forcade bought us down to a shaky landing near a cluster of artificial domes. These were coloured in various shades of red, yellow and blue, making them look against the dusty monochrome landscape like carnival balloons at a funeral. I don't mean that in a bad way, by the way – I've left strict instructions that my own funeral should last for at least a week and involve balloons, helter-skelters and bouncy castles. Not small ones, mind you. Castle-sized ones.

When he cracked the airlock, and I could smell something apart from my own very exclusive perfume and Forcade's rather emphatic aftershave, I noticed that the planet actually smelled old as well. There was something musty, rusty and probably other words ending with '-ty' that I can't think of at the moment in the atmosphere. It's a smell that all ancient worlds get, after a while. Even if I'd been blindfolded (and I didn't know the Professor well enough for that) I would have known that this planet predated most of inhabited space.

Emerging from the spacecraft, we met with Professor Forcade's archaeological team. There were perhaps twenty of them, but five minutes after they were introduced I could only remember two of their names. One was Paul Markol – a thin man with dark skin, brown eyes and a permanent frown who hadn't bathed for a while. The other was Sonja Toulder: shorter but wider than Markol, with blonde hair and black eyebrows. I've probably met several hundreds of thousands of people over the course of however many lifetimes I've lived to date, and I've discovered that there's no point using up storage space in my brain for their names when it would be more fun and more useful to remember as many cocktail recipes as possible. Everybody, I decided a long time ago, I would just call 'Sweetie' unless for some reason my brain decided to lodge their names in some spot that used to contain the ingredients for a Gumblejack Surprise (which, by the way, is one of the cocktails I don't want to remember).

Both Markol and Toulder looked at me like I might whip a semi-automatic laser out of my clutch bag and gun them down with it. They'd obviously heard about Stormcage. Honestly, if they knew anything about me then they'd know I was much more likely to pull out my bottle of champagne and some party poppers and start the fun. Then use the laser when everyone had passed out drunk.

After the rather tense introductions, the three of them led me across to the huge door that I had seen on the comp-paper back at Stormcage. In context I could see that it was in a ziggurat-like building in the centre of the plaza. It was open now, but the weak light from the sun didn't penetrate far inside. The vast scale of the opening made me feel small, although for the Qwerm it would have been quite cosy, I suspect.

Spotlights on poles had been placed just inside the doorway. Markol pressed a button on a remote control he retrieved from his coveralls and the lights came on.

I gasped, even though part of me had already suspected what the Professor and his team had found.

In the middle of the shadowy space inside the bunker, like a child's building block in the middle of a dining room, was a blue box. It was about eight feet tall and four feet wide, and it had frosted windows. And a door. And a sign running along the top that said, in white letters on a black background, 'Police Public Call Box'. Another sign, this time black letters on a white background, was placed at chest-height on a door at the front.

As I walked closer I could see that this sign said:

> In the event that this box is found,
> Please return to Professor River Song
> c/o the Stormcage Penal Facility

Now that I hadn't been expecting.

I had to break off my last entry, because Professor Forcade wanted to have a team meeting, which was cleverly combined with a team meal. The food was tasteless, and the portions were so small as well! He had to catch up on what had happened since he'd left for Stormcage, and he also wanted to introduce me to the team (I was fabulous, by the way). There was a lot of talk about what they had found, and the fact that my name was on it. I tried to persuade them all that I'm as puzzled by the appearance of the TARDIS, and the fact that it's got my contact details on its front, as they are, but I suspect that some of them think that I'm lying. Markol certainly thinks I am – he glowers at me in a very unfriendly way. Toulder and the other sweeties seem to want to give me the benefit of the doubt.

I did notice some strange little tics that the team displayed, as they sat around the conference table in one of their prefab domes. A lot of them seemed preoccupied with their necks – pulling at their collars and scratching at their skin. I also noticed that some of them were wearing their coveralls buttoned right up to the neck (it's not a good look, in any culture), and there were indications that the skin underneath was inflamed. I have filed that all away for separate consideration. The Doctor would probably have taken all of the observations and built them into an edifice of truth, but despite the time I'd spent with him, and the fact that I was a child of the TARDIS, I couldn't do what he did. Nobody else in the universe could, I suspect.

Despite my protestations at the staff meeting, I've been racking my brains for reasons why the TARDIS might be here, in the middle of an ancient alien ziggurat on a planet on the neglected outskirts of the galaxy. Has it just arrived, or has it been here for a while? Are my mum and dad here as well? Is the Doctor inside, or is he off exploring? Is it something to do with the ancient campaigns that the Time Lords waged against the more dangerous races of their time, or an accidental conflation of two separate things? Why does pink go with black, but not with navy blue? I realised early on in my life that the universe is full of questions to which I may never get the answers.

Oh, what I didn't mention earlier is that the TARDIS is sitting in a wide circle of some kind of dust. I know I said that the planet itself is dusty, which it is, but this dust is different. It's yellow, and it seems to shimmer in the light of the lamps. If you catch sight of it in the corner of your eye, it almost looks like it's vibrating very slightly. I don't think I've ever seen anything quite like it.

Anyway, it's late now, and I've been awake for quite a while. I think it's time to put the questions to bed and get some beauty sleep. I don't need it, of course – I look fabulous under any and all circumstances – but it's always wise to keep it topped up because you never know when you might run short.

After all, it's not as if I can regenerate my way out of wrinkles any more. I used that little trick up in Nazi Germany in the 1930s. Now all I have to save my looks is good genes and a comprehensive moisturising regime.

Well, this has been a day to remember.

There's something about waking up and finding yourself being carried through the open air by things you can't see that really puts a crimp in a girl's night. Whatever they were, they had my arms, my legs and my neck held tightly, and they were moving fast across the plaza. I couldn't see what they were because I was facing the sparsely starred night sky. There were three moons in sight, but two of them seemed to have been half-destroyed in some ancient attack. The things they were grasping me with felt like claws, and I could hear the clicking of hard-shelled legs against the stone of the plaza. Groggily, I wondered if I'd been kidnapped by a tribe of large crabs. Obviously, it wasn't the Qwerm. Not unless they had (a) survived when they were supposed to have died out, and (b) got a lot smaller over the millennia. Still the Macra had got a lot larger, so who knows?

My head was muzzy. I had probably been drugged. Something in the food, maybe? I suspect I woke up before I was supposed to, largely thanks to the lipstick I wear. Over the years it's given me a partial immunity to anaesthetics and paralysing drugs.

I heard more clicking from somewhere near. I turned my head, and saw that Professor Forcade was being carried alongside me. He looked confused and outraged at the same time, but I was actually more interested in what was holding him up. It was members of his team. Or, rather, it was their heads.

It took me a few moments to actually work out what was going on. Imagine that someone's head has come off, and sprouted eight glossy black legs and a large set of glossy black claws, a bit like giant crabs, or enormous lice. Imagine them scuttling across the ground, claws held high. Oh, and imagine that on the other side of their heads to their faces, instead of hair, there are now other, alien faces, made up of multiple black eyes and twitching, grasping mouthparts. That's what I was looking at.

Head-lice. The thought suddenly struck me, and despite the fear that was gripping my heart I giggled. Forcade looked at me as if I was mad.

The blonde woman with the black roots – Toulder – was one of the head-lice. She glared at me with eyes from which all the humanity had been drained.

I really hoped that this was a nightmare, but the rapid beating of my heart, the pinching of the claws on my skin and the breeze across my face suggested that it wasn't. Besides, most of my nightmares revolve around me turning up naked to a party, which is funny because many of the parties I go to end up the other way around.

'What's happening?' Professor Forcade shouted.

'We're being kidnapped by giant crustaceans that used to be the heads of your archaeological team!' I called back. I spent three years back on Earth as a management consultant, back when I was young and black. I'm very good at answering people's questions with things they already know, and then charging a fortune for the service.

'What do they want?' His face indicated that he was on the verge of panic.

'Us, obviously.'

Raising my head and looking around, I realised that the head-lice were taking us towards the ziggurat in the middle of which the TARDIS was sitting. I knew I had to do something before we got there. I managed to wrestle my right arm free from the claws of one of the creatures. I wiped my fingers across my mouth, then reached down and smeared my lipstick across its black hard-shelled back.

The solvent that I'd recently introduced into the recipe, along with the vivid scarlet dye and the hint of sparkle, only took a few seconds to take effect. It started with a shrill noise from the creature I'd touched, a sound that mixed the worst parts of a scream and a dentist's drill. It suddenly released me and veered sideways, waving its claws frantically in the air.

I reached behind my back like a contortionist (I'm very flexible) and brushed the legs of the creature that was holding my left arm tight with my lipstick-sticky fingers. The creature started to wobble, and I heard a fizzing noise followed by the lovely clatter of its legs falling off, one after the other. It let me go, and with both arms free I was able to wipe my lipstick onto the shells of all the remaining ones. They let me fall to the ground and ran off on random paths. One or two just rushed around in circles. The red lipstick ('Scarlet Sin', I think it was called) fizzed and bubbled on their metal casings. Their human heads were fixed in expressions of agony, and their black-lensed eyes seemed to be staring in horror.

I went to rescue the Professor, but the head-lice carrying him dropped him to the ground and fled.

'Thank you!' he gasped.

'They should count themselves lucky I haven't got any blusher with me,' I responded. Grabbing his arm I started running towards the ziggurat.

'That's where they were taking us!' he cried, pulling away.

'I know,' I said, 'but it's defensible, and besides – don't you want to see what they were taking us to do?'

He was gazing back over his shoulder in shock. 'I don't understand any of this. What happened to them? What do they want from us?'

'Priorities, Professor – answers can come after survival,' I said firmly, 'and we haven't assured our survival yet. Now come on.'

We ran into the shadows, towards the TARDIS. I turned and looked at the glyphs carved into the frame of the doorway on the inside. There, about twenty feet from the ground, was the one that closed the door. I scrambled up, using the outsized lower glyphs as ledges for my hands and feet, and threw my weight against the control one. It slid in a few inches and lit up with a flickering orange light, and the door ponderously closed, leaving us in darkness.

I found my way by memory to where the TARDIS stood. As I got closer, the light on top flickered hesitantly into life. It knew me.

I pushed against the door, and it swung open with a creak.

Professor Forcade appeared at my shoulder. He gazed into the TARDIS's interior in wonder and terror.

The first thing I realised was that this wasn't the Doctor's TARDIS, despite the out-of-place exterior appearance and the sign on the door. He changes the look as often as I change my hairstyle, and for pretty much the same reasons, but he has a certain brooding, gothic style and I could tell that this wasn't one of his designs.

The entrance opened onto a stairway that went upwards, through the space also occupied by the roof and the blue light. The stairs were made of white marble with rose-coloured inclusions: a classic style that never looks old, I've found. Professor Forcade started burbling. I squeezed his hand in reassurance.

'I know – it's impossible,' I said as I closed the door behind us to keep the head-lice things out. 'Get over it.'

There were seventeen steps leading up to an opening in the floor of... something. When we emerged from the opening I realised that we were just off-centre in the base of a white sphere so large you probably could have fitted a small moon inside, or indeed my complete collection of shoes. The dimensionally transcendent interior of this TARDIS had apparently been reconfigured into a single space. The point marking the exact base of the sphere was the console itself: a hexagonal mushroom-shape that appeared to have been chiselled out of white marble as well.

'Is this... Precursor technology?' the Professor asked. 'Did we pass through some kind of portal into a different space?'

'Not entirely.' I shrugged. 'It's all to do with dimensional squeezing, or so I'm told.'

If the vast white sphere of the TARDIS's interior had actually been empty then I would have been able to make a much better estimate of its true size, but it wasn't empty. It was filled with fuzzy white oblong shapes that were strung together by cobwebs as thick as a person. The white of the objects against the white of the TARDIS interior made it difficult to tell how big they were but it looked to me like they were each as big as Professor Forcade's spaceship. They hung in all orientations – vertical, horizontal, diagonal – but the cobwebby material seemed to link them by their ends. In effect, there were long strands of these things criss-crossing the void, like bizarre Christmas decorations strung in impossibly long lines.

'What are they?' Forcade breathed.

'I have a horrible feeling,' I said.

'They look like... giant chrysalises,' he went on. Honestly, some people just don't know when to leave well enough alone.

'Yes,' I said. 'That was my horrible feeling.'

He scratched his neck. 'But how could—'

'Sshhh,' I said, raising a finger to his lips. He stopped speaking, and I listened intently. With the great Time Engines of this TARDIS having been silent for a million years there should have been no noise in there, but I could hear a rustling, far far away. It sounded like the wind brushing its way through piles of dry leaves, but I suspected that it had a much more unpleasant source.

I suspected that some of these chrysalises were close to hatching, but how could that be true after so long? There were things here I just didn't understand.

I've seen things that have scared me before. I've faced Weeping Angels and the Silents; I've faced Daleks and Cybermen and the Crimson Revenants. I know what fear feels like, and I know how not to show it, because if you show the things you're scared of that you are scared then that gives them more power (certainly true in the case of the Crimson Revenants, who eat fear and excrete sheer terror in return). Mostly I can control my feelings, either because I'm with people I trust or because I can see a clear way out. But here, and now... the scale of what I was looking at terrified me. Millions of Qwerm chrysalises, ready to hatch. Millions of them and one of me. What could I do?

I turned away from Professor Forcade so he couldn't see the panic that I could feel on my face. I found myself looking back towards the console at the base of the sphere – which I was now thinking of as a cross between a giant ancient nursery and a giant ancient hive – but I caught a flash of something different from behind some of the cocoons that were near the floor. I gingerly led the way over, manoeuvring my way past their cotton-wool surfaces, which rose up around us like gently curved and rather woolly cliff faces. The cobwebby substance that linked them together and held them up looked fragile, but I did my best not to touch it. I once saw a man try to brush his way through a web of monomolecular fibres (let's not go into where or why right now). Everything from his fingertips to his elbows suddenly turned into something resembling roughly chopped salami. It wasn't pleasant, and I didn't want the same thing happening to me.

In a clear space between the cocoons we came across the body of a Qwerm. I'd never seen one before, but there was no doubt about what it was. As the legends said, it was long and locust-like, and big enough that it could have occupied the space of five or six shops in any high street you care to name. What I hadn't expected was that its hard exterior skin was black, and gleamed like oiled metal. It had drawn its legs up towards its underside when it had died. Everything inside should have rotted away or dried out over the millennia, but it looked as though it might just stretch out and move off at a moment's notice.

Professor Forcade seemed shocked into silence. That was probably a good thing. Gibbering never looks good in a man.

I moved around to the front of the Qwerm. Its head was the same size as the Mini Cooper I used to drive, back when I was young, when my parents were my best friends and when I only had one goal in life – to kill the Doctor. Its eyes were like massive, faceted obsidian gemstones, but there was no gleam of life in them. The various complicated mouthparts – which I suspect also would have doubled as manipulators, like hands or tentacles in other species, hung limply from its maw.

They still had traces of biological fluid on them. That wasn't a good sign.

'What... what killed it?' Forcade whispered.

'Like millions of human women through history,' I replied, gazing up at the chrysalises up hanging in near-infinite array above us, 'it died in childbirth.'

Forcade moved closed to the dried-out husk of the Qwerm. I was just about to warn him not to touch it, but he leant forwards, hands behind his back, and gazed closely at something between two of the metallic plates that made up its body. Suddenly he sprang back, hands raised in defence.

'They've found us again!' he cried.

I moved closer cautiously. It's something I learned from the Doctor: always move towards danger rather than away from it – it's the last thing they'll expect. I used to ask him who 'they' were, but he'd just look at me in exasperation and say, 'It's a metaphorical "they". "They" as in "the personification of whatever is causing the danger".'

'But why "they"?' I'd press him. 'Why not "he" or "she" or "it"?'

'Because danger always comes with reinforcements,' he'd say.

What Forcade had found looked initially like some kind of growth or protrusion from the soft tissues inside the shell, but as I got closer I realised that it looked a lot like the head-lice that had abducted us outside, on the planet's surface: a shell roughly the size of a human skull, eight organic hard-shelled legs and two pincers. The legs and the pincers were curled up beneath it now, and the shell wasn't actually a head – just the same size as one. It had eyes like black lenses set into things that looked like organic goggles, and multiple mouthparts, like the Qwerm.

'What is it?' Forcade asked nervously. 'Some kind of parasite?'

'More like a mutually beneficial partner,' I ventured. Looking over the massive black bulk of the Qwerm, I saw another four or five creatures just the same, nestled between its plates. 'I suspect these things did a lot of the fetching and carrying for the Qwerm. I'm not sure what they got back in return, however – maybe some kind of secretion from the Qwerm's body that they used as nourishment?'

Forcade glanced nervously at the stairs. 'But why does it look like those... things... that my team have turned into?'

'I don't know,' I replied, 'but I don't think it's a coincidence.'

'When the Qwerm have no servants,' a dry, whispering voice said, 'they must make new ones.'

The sound was shocking in the dense silence created by the cocoons and the cobwebs. We both turned. I think the Professor might have weed himself just a little.

The voice was coming from the TARDIS's console. We moved cautiously around the bulk of the dead Qwerm and the various chrysalises on the floor until we could see it properly.

I gasped, and the Professor made a choking noise.

I hadn't noticed before, but the centre bit of the console – the time rotor, as the Doctor used to call it – had been removed. Protruding from it was the head and chest of... well, I wasn't sure. It had to be a Time Lord, but it looked like one who had been caught impossibly in the middle of a regeneration. The left side was an old woman with close-cropped silver hair, one blue eye and deep lines on her face, but the right side was a girl, maybe 10 years old, with long brown hair and one green eye. The two halves of the head were the same size, more or less, with a kind of rough, lumpy dividing line between them, as if the body's incredible Time Lord metabolism had tried to make the best of a bad job but not done very well.

Strands of the cobwebby stuff shrouded her body, and led away into the vast space of the TARDIS. It was as if she was attached to the chrysalises by the ancient ghosts of cables and wires.

'Hello,' I said, trying to keep my voice steady. 'Who are you?'

'I won't tell you my real name,' she replied softly, 'but some people used to call me Rocinante.' Her voice started out old and cracked, but gradually segued into something younger and more hesitant as she spoke.

'How long have you been in here?' Forcade asked. His eyes were wide. I wasn't sure how much more of this he could take. If it came to that, I wasn't sure how much more of this I could take.

'For me, a few weeks,' she said. Her eyes were brown and her hair was fair, only slightly darker than the cobwebs. 'For the universe outside, I don't know. Maybe a million years.'

'Ah,' I said, realising. 'A time field.'

She nodded. 'The Qwerm made me switch it on after they had filled the TARDIS with their larvae.'

'Of course.' I nodded. 'It's all so obvious.'

'Not to me,' Forcade protested. He was pulling the collar of his coveralls away from his skin as if something underneath was irritating him.

'It's all to do with the ancient clearances,' I explained in my best lecturer's voice. 'The Time Lords had allied themselves with the Qwerm and others to fight the Racnoss, the Great Vampires and whatever other races wanted to sweep across the universe like a plague and destroy everything, but once the clearances were over the Time Lords looked around and realised they'd made a new generation of problems. Races like the Qwerm had militarised themselves, and they couldn't go back. With nothing left to fight, what would they do?'

'The Qwerm were incredibly intelligent,' the pale girl whispered. 'Five brains, all operating in parallel. They knew that they would be next on the list, so they devised a plan. They would capture a TARDIS from one of their Time Lord advisers, lay billions of eggs inside that TARDIS, then leave it hidden in a time field until the universe had calmed down and pacified itself, until the Time Lords had sunk into the complacency that affects all great empires, and they could hatch out and sweep across the universe. To the victors, the spoils. That was their attitude. They felt they had earned the right to the universe.' She smiled, but on one side of her face it looked bitter and the other side radiant.

'This is that TARDIS,' I said, 'and you are that Time Lord adviser.'

She glanced around at the cobwebs – or Qwerm power and data conduits, as I now realised they were – that strung her up. I followed the cables with my eyes. They linked her not to any Qwerm technology that I could see but to the cocoons themselves. I glanced back at her, and saw that she was looking at me thoughtfully.

'The Racnoss are born hungry,' she said quietly. 'That's what they say. Or said, anyway. In contrast, the Qwerm are born thinking. Even in their chrysalises, they are planning and considering and sifting evidence. And I'm linked to them now. Part of them. I can sense their thoughts, and their intentions, and they can force me to do things for them.' She hesitated, shaking her head slightly. The hair over the younger side of her face swung in front of her eyes.

'And what about...' I gestured at the two sides of her body, at the old, scrawny arm on one side, like a gnarled tree root and the young limb on the other.

'The pain of what they did, using me as an interface between my TARDIS and themselves, forcing me to set up the time field by the sheer weight of their minds, caused me to regenerate,' she continued sadly, 'but the time field switched on while I was in the middle of changing. Half of my body refreshed itself, and half stayed as it was. When the Professor's archaeology team discovered my TARDIS it woke up, the time field collapsed, and I found myself like this – neither one thing nor another. Caught in between two different bodies.'

Professor Forcade's face was white and strained. He was still tugging at his collar. 'This is all very well, but what does this have to do with what happened out there?' he asked, waving vaguely at the stairs. 'I suppose I can accept that the Qwerm have left their larvae frozen in a time field for a millennium, but how did that affect my team?'

'And me,' I pointed out. 'Not that I want to make out that everything is about me, although it is, but why was my name on the front of this TARDIS, and why did it look like..?' I hesitated, leaving the words 'the Doctor's TARDIS' unsaid.

'Someone needed to open the front door,' she said. 'The last thing I managed to do of my own free will before the time field was established was to trigger the emergency war protocols, established in case of compromise of a TARDIS or a Time Lord. It didn't matter that eventually the time field would collapse: my TARDIS was sealed and could only be opened by another of my race.' She smiled at me, sweetly. 'Or a child of a TARDIS. That I did not foresee. You were lured here. Once my TARDIS recognised the mark of the Time Vortex in your DNA, it unlocked itself for you.'

'Lured how?' I was fascinated by Rocinante's story, but at the same time I was aware that the rustling noises high above us were getting more intense.

'Once this TARDIS was discovered by the Professor's archaeology team, the time field collapsed and my TARDIS was freed. It could link in to any communications system in range. It could link in to other TARDISes in the current time zone, wherever they are in the universe, and siphon off what they know.'

'TARDISes can't do that,' I pointed out.

'They used to be able to. We had something we called the Vortex Web. It linked all of our TARDISes together for tactical planning and communications purposes. The capability is still there, but apparently nobody uses it any more.' She smiled shyly on half of her face. 'That's how the Qwerm larvae hive mind, linked through me to my TARDIS, found out about this fascinating person called the Doctor, and about you. It set a trap. It used the chameleon circuit to alter the outside of my TARDIS to look like this Doctor's broken TARDIS, and the sign on the front to make sure that it was you, rather than him, who would be lured here. The Qwerm larval hive mind decided that you would be less dangerous than him.' She cocked her head to one side, and grimaced. 'I'm sorry. That was their assessment, not mine.'

'And the archaeological team?'

'The Qwerm larval hive mind needed servants to find you and bring you here. My TARDIS was surrounded by dormant microbe-sized robots.'

'The yellow powder,' I said quietly, kicking myself for not having realised earlier.

'They infiltrated the bodies of the team through their air passages and their lungs and adjusted them... rebuilt them... to a form that was more familiar to the Qwerm, similar to their old servants from hundreds of billions of years ago. As I said, when the Qwerm have no servants, they must make more servants.'

'And now what?' I asked. 'The Time Lords didn't die out, you know? They're still around, and they won't stand for this.' It was bravado, but I was hoping Rocinante, and more importantly the Qwerm larvae who were listening to us through her ears, didn't know that.

I was wrong.

'According to the history that my TARDIS has downloaded from the Vortex Web,' she said, 'the Time Lords are old and decrepit now. Their time has gone. Their one chance at redeeming themselves and recapturing their old glories in this Time War failed, and they have hidden themselves away in another dimension somewhere. They will not stop us.'

'Us?' I queried.

'The Qwerm,' she corrected herself, frowning. 'In fact, once the Qwerm take control of the universe, as is their right, they might well invite the Time Lords to join them. As junior partners, of course. For old times' sake.'

'How sweet,' I said.

Rocinante opened her mouth to say something, but there was a sudden crashing from nearby. I whirled round, to see one of the chrysalises falling to the bottom of the sphere of the TARDIS's interior, bouncing off the webbing that criss-crossed the space as it went. The chrysalis had a long tear in its side, where something had climbed out.

And above our heads I thought I could see something oily and black moving around uncertainly, clutching at the webbing for support with claws the size of my whole body.

'They're hatching,' Rocinante whispered. Half of her face was twisted in terror, but the other half was gazing upwards in exultation.

Another chrysalis crashed down, almost covering the stairs that we had entered through, and which were our only chance to get out.

Or were they?

I remembered something that the Doctor had once let slip. If Rule One is that the Doctor lies then Rule Two is that he often says things that aren't true just for comedic purposes and Rule Three is that even when he's not lying and not joking then he's often wrong, but it was the only chance I could see. The only thing that could stop an army of gigantic super-intelligent space locusts from ravaging the universe.

A third empty cocoon fell towards the console, ending up caught in a cat's-cradle of webbing ten feet above Rocinante's head. She hardly seemed to notice.

Half of her was paralysed with fear; half was paralysed in near-religious ecstasy.

I glanced over at Professor Forcade. My mouth was just opening to say, 'I'm going to need your help with this,' when I noticed that he was staring at me oddly. Blankly, as if he didn't recognise me. And then his entire head lifted off his neck, supported by eight hard-shelled legs, while two claws unfolded from beneath his jaw.

I'd known that it was only a matter of time before the Qwerm nanobots managed to infect him. They had probably infected me too, except that I was hoping that my genetic inheritance as a child of the TARDIS would prevent them from functioning.

Forcade's body fell to the curved floor while his head made a leap for the nearest strands of webbing and scuttled away, clicking its claws at me and staring balefully through clusters of eyes on what had been the back of its head. I wasn't going to be getting any help from him either.

I moved quickly across to the console. I'd watched the Doctor enough times to know what to do and what not to do – which was usually the opposite of what he did and what he didn't do. Quickly, almost instinctively, my hands flickered over the controls.

'What... what are you doing?' Rocinante asked in a voice that swung disconcertingly between old age and youth.

'The Doctor once told me,' I said, still working frantically away, 'that all TARDISes have not only a front door but also a back door, for use in emergencies.'

I glanced upwards. Several vast and iridescent black shapes were moving towards me from different directions.

'What I am doing,' I went on, 'is connecting the front door to the back door in something called an infinite Klein bottle. Anyone or anything leaving through the front door will find themselves coming in through the front door. This TARDIS will become a sealed system.'

Cocoons were splitting all across the astronomical expanse of the TARDIS's internal space now. Thousands, maybe tens of thousands of Qwerm were being born even as I watched.

'You'll be trapped in here,' Rocinante gasped.

'My original intention was that the Professor would press the final switch just as I made it through the doors,' I said grimly, 'which would have been good for me and the universe but not so good for the Professor. That isn't going to work now. I never thought that this was how I would end up, but hey! We all have to go some time.'

The ancient part of Rocinante's face glared at me murderously, but the lips of the child side curved into a childish smile. 'Run,' she said. 'Let me handle that final switch.'

'Are you sure?'

'I'm sure.' She wrenched her arm from the grip of the webbing and reached down towards the console.

'Thank you,' I said.

I ran for the stairs as fast as I could. I fell down them, and rolled through the open doors. As they slammed shut behind me I saw, just for a moment, the whole of the space inside wrap back on itself.

I still had to get past the head-lice before I could find safe refuge in Professor Forcade's spacecraft, of course, but compared to what I'd already accomplished that was child's play. They didn't seem to know what was going on, and kicking them away as I ran made a satisfying crunching sound. It did ruin my shoes, but that can easily be fixed. I had gone through a hellish experience, but the only therapy I needed was of the retail variety.

Kanenda Station, here I come.

I came back to Stormcage in the end, of course. It wasn't as if I really had any choice. The Governor still has my vortex manipulator in her possession, and if I want to see my mother and father and my husband any more then I will need it. So, after an extended shopping spree and a number of parties I piloted the Professor's spacecraft back to the grim, rain-lashed planet that I had come to regard as home.

I don't think the Governor was pleased to see me, despite the fact that I had returned of my own accord. She wanted to know what had happened to Professor Forcade, but I didn't particularly want to share that story, so I kept quiet (which isn't like me at all). She withdrew all of my privileges and stripped my cell of all the books and pictures I had accumulated over the course of my incarceration. She also banned me from seeing or talking to anyone else, including the wardens.

So, here I sit, memorising my own diary entries so that I can write them down properly when I get my journal back. It doesn't matter. Having time to myself to think is good. Having a lot of time to myself means I can do a lot of thinking.

The arthropods that live in the cracks in my cell walls have come up with some interesting ideas for getting my vortex manipulator back. Once we've worked out all the kinks, we'll put their plan into effect.

BBC

DOCTOR WHO

Royal Blood

Una McCormack

ISBN 978 1 84990 992 1

The Grail is a story, a myth! It didn't exist on your world! It can't exist here!

The city-state of Varuz is failing. Duke Aurelian is the last
of his line, his capital is crumbling, and the armies of his enemy,
Duke Conrad, are poised beyond the mountains to invade.
Aurelian is preparing to gamble everything on one last battle.
So when a holy man, the Doctor, comes to Varuz from beyond
the mountains, Aurelian asks for his blessing in the war.

But all is not what it seems in Varuz. The city-guard have
lasers for swords, and the halls are lit by electric candlelight.
Aurelian's beloved wife, Guena, and his most trusted knight,
Bernhardt, seem to be plotting to overthrow their Duke,
and Clara finds herself drawn into their intrigue…

Will the Doctor stop Aurelian from going to war?
Will Clara's involvement in the plot against the Duke
be discovered? Why is Conrad's ambassador so nervous?
And who are the ancient and weary knights who arrive
in Varuz claiming to be on a quest for the Holy Grail…?

*An original novel featuring the Twelfth Doctor and Clara,
as played by Peter Capaldi and Jenna Coleman*

B B C

DOCTOR WHO

Big Bang Generation

Gary Russell

ISBN 978 1 84990 991 4

I'm an archaeologist, but probably not the one you were expecting.

Christmas 2015, Sydney, New South Wales, Australia

Imagine everyone's surprise when a time portal opens up in Sydney Cove. Imagine their shock as a massive pyramid now sits beside the Harbour Bridge, inconveniently blocking Port Jackson and glowing with energy. Imagine their fear as Cyrrus 'the mobster' Globb, Professor Horace Jaanson and an alien assassin called Kik arrive to claim the glowing pyramid. Finally imagine everyone's dismay when they are followed by a bunch of con artists out to spring their greatest grift yet.

This gang consists of Legs (the sexy comedian), Dog Boy (providing protection and firepower), Shortie (handling logistics), Da Trowel (in charge of excavation and history) and their leader, Doc (busy making sure the universe isn't destroyed in an explosion that makes the Big Bang look like a damp squib).

And when someone accidentally reawakens The Ancients of the Universe – which, Doc reckons, wasn't the wisest or best-judged of actions – things get a whole lot more complicated…

An original novel featuring the Twelfth Doctor, as played by Peter Capaldi

BBC

DOCTOR WHO

Deep Time

Trevor Baxendale

ISBN 978 1 84990 990 7

I do hope you're all ready to be terrified!

The Phaeron disappeared from the universe over a million years ago.
They travelled among the stars using roads made from time and space,
but left only relics behind. But what actually happened to the Phaeron?

In the far future, humans discover the location of the last Phaeron
road – and the Doctor and Clara join the mission to see where the road
leads. Each member of the research team knows exactly what they're
looking for – but only the Doctor knows exactly what they'll find.

Because only the Doctor knows the true secret of the Phaeron: a
monstrous secret so terrible and powerful that it must be buried
in the deepest grave imaginable…

*An original novel featuring the Twelfth Doctor and Clara, as played by Peter
Capaldi and Jenna Coleman*